The Adventures *of* Link Lawrence

John L. Bowman

The Adventures of Link Lawrence

ISBN 979-8-218-54239-9

CONTENTS

I.   THE ADVENTURE

II.   ENLIGHTENMENT AND NATURE

III.   PHILOSOPHY, NATURE, CIVILIZATION AND HAPPINESS

PART 1 - THE ADVENTURE

Chapter 1

Probatis

My life could not have been worse. It was like a surreal nightmare, as if I were imprisoned in Dante's *Inferno,* tightly bound and suspended in the air, upside down, slowly roasting over a hot burning fire, suffering horrible pain, or Prometheus chained to a rock by Zeus with buzzards eternally eating his liver. It was like the Fate Clotho, called the Spinner because she wove human destinies, hated men and took her goddess anger out on me. To make my pain worse, wickedly she poured honey over my charring body and covered me with fire ants. My life was one of insufferable torture. But my physical pain was nothing compared to my mental angst.

I was the unfortunate runt born into an impoverished family living in the slums in a city named Probatis in a country called Utopianus. My father, Malcolm Laurence, was a mean-spirited, violent, and brutal man who beat me often, and my mother, Olivia Laurence, formerly a prostitute, resented my existence. Neither of them loved me.

Dad left when I was very young, and I left Mom when I was in my early teens and lived on the street. I had two awful older sisters who treated me with contempt. Mede was a violently anti-male alcoholic and Moppen, a haughty prig.

I suppose I could be called an odd character living an odd life that only got odder in my youth, yet a life that ironically became interesting as I aged. My first life trauma was caused by a confused eighth-grade teacher who told me that even though I looked and acted like a boy, I was really a girl. Without informing Mom, who couldn't have cared less, she steered me into an indoctrination program that told me my genes and hormones were wrong, and I needed estrogen hormone therapy and transgender surgery. I was young and confused because I thought old people were wise. However, intuitively I told myself to go slow because it is probably a growing phase, like a young tomboy girl. Sure enough, with puberty, my male hormones kicked in, I grew a beard, my voice deepened, I got bigger, I started having wet dreams, and the misguided teacher disappeared. I often wondered what would have happened if I had been castrated and made an unnatural and probably troubled young woman. I also wondered how many young people that that teacher had tragically mutilated, damaging them for life.

My short time in high school was miserable. I had no friends due to my petulantly combative personality, and I was often suspended for fighting. Because I had acne and was gangly and scrawny, the girls shunned me. Once, I got the courage to ask a girl out, only to hear giggling in the background and a girl whisper, "Ugh, you were asked out by ugly Link," before she turned me down. From then on, I never asked another girl out or went to a school dance. I was a pariah and just gave up.

In high school, I wanted to learn and go to college, but I was not much of a student and had no encouragement or money, so I dropped out my sophomore year and got a job as a janitor. When I was seventeen, I had sex for the first time, with Freya Miller, a homeless girl, who immediately got pregnant. Freya refused to get an abortion and insisted I marry her. So, at a young age, I was trapped by a conniving Theodora into an unhappy marriage, obliged to support a family I did not want and could not afford. I suspected at the time that my life was not getting off to the most auspicious start.

Freya and I had two children: Emily, a rebel who got pregnant at thirteen, and Duncan, who became a worthless meth addict at fifteen. Both hated me because Freya told them I was the source of all their problems. I could not afford a house, so we lived in a degraded and dangerously dilapidated government-subsidized apartment complex amongst violent gangs, prostitutes, and drug addicts. There were nightly shootings, and usually a dead body in the street in the morning.

I wasn't making enough money to support everyone and was tired of poverty and aggressive bill collectors, so I quit my janitor job and started work at Sweet Bucket as a sanitary engineer. It was worse than jumping from the frying pan into the fire; it was like jumping from the toilet bowl into a putrid cesspool. I drove a truck, serviced portable toilets, and managed feces. It was an awful, boring, dirty, low-paying, dead-end job that made me feel and smell like shit that repulsed my family. When I returned tired from a long day's work, they usually left, gasping on their way out the door.

As a toilet cleaner "untouchable," all of society looked down on me. I was one rung above a pedophile in the social pecking order. People ignored, ridiculed, and openly disparaged me. Because of others' disrespect, I developed a number of physical and mental maladies. A few of the physical illnesses were addiction to alcohol, chronic heartburn, headaches, and a nervous lisp. I will describe my mental ones shortly. My civil life in class-conscious Probatis was dreadful.

Freya turned out to be a shrewish, controlling, highly critical wife. She constantly belittled me for our poverty and always said marrying me was her life's greatest mistake. After a few years of marriage, she cheated on me, left with the kids, and we divorced. At this time, my life looked utterly bleak and hopeless, and I dreaded having to live it.

When I was young, my odd personality was hyper, edgy, and nervous, mostly due to civilization. I was one of those people who had many bad experiences, some of which actually happened-I had legions of imaginary fears that kept me constantly wary and defensive. I did not trust other people and would always abandon them before they had the chance to abandon me. I had no friends or close relationships. My fears also made me religious at times. I was a devout High Church Catholic, mostly due to Pascal's Wager to believe just in case it is true. I was also clumsy, unskilled, and unathletic. In high school, I tried out for the track team, did not pace myself in my first mile, was exhausted, slowed to a stumble after the first lap, and came in dead last. Predictably, I did not make the team.

Society also robbed me of my self-esteem. Because I was despised, I felt inferior and lacked confidence. To compensate for this, I became an iconoclast, questioning the value of civilization and an unabashed Epicurean pleasure seeker. Being a dissipated aggressor somehow made me feel strong and worthy because I was abusing someone else. I pursued fine food, sexual pleasure, and alcohol with abandon. I was a satisfied pig. Also, unbeknownst to me then, I was happily ignorant. My array of knowledge was microscopic.

The upshot of all this made me mildly schizophrenic. On one hand, I was closed and guarded, but on the other, I felt open and free. Most of the time, I would retreat into my mental redoubt, but as I got older, some deep, inner urge would occasionally push me forcefully into the world.

On top of my miserable personal life, society was crumbling all around me, my world was increasingly strange, and I was becoming an alien in my own time. Utopianus and Probatis were originally ordered clean and safe, but over time they became chaotic, dirty, and dangerous. It is hard to say why, but as strange as this may sound, democracy was a cause. Democracy, the shining beacon of freedom, faded because I think humans cannot handle the freedom it brings. Fallible people seem incapable of understanding that with freedom comes responsibility. Immorality, socialism, and divisiveness emerged, and the infrastructure began crumbling. Some very strange movements arose, like the politically correct cancel culture and imperious woke, both aspects of the "thought police." There also began an insane movement to defund the police, which only made crime spike. Over time, my country, Utopianus, became Dystopianus, and my city, Probatis, became Decadere.

Certainly, other society-rending events contributed to the decline. The war in Asia, the vagabond hippy culture championed by Kerouac, Ginsburg, and Leary, and the spirit of the time's slogans—sex, drugs, and rock and roll—also assailed the fabric of a stable society. My city was like a sandbar in a river slowly being eroded by strong, aimless currents.

My depressing existence had confused and confounded young, uneducated me—I felt awful and did not know what to do. I finally decided there was nothing for me in my hometown or in the life Clotho had spun for me, so I took a leap of faith and left. I was scared to death because I had never been anywhere beyond Probatis, but I was energized and excited to escape and see what fortune offered me in spite of Clotho. I must tell you, despite my early life challenges, circumstances and disappointments, to my astonishment, my life gradually changed for the better.

My name is Link Lawrence. Link was the name of a video game my parents liked, and Lawrence is our family's Scottish surname that ironically means *bright* or *shining one*. Like Johnny Cash's *Sue*, when I was young, I was teased unmercifully because of my name, so I changed my first name to Albert and, over time, added some middle names for disguise. I added Zamperini because I liked his book about being adrift at sea for 47 days on a life raft, Irwin, after the famous adventurer Steve Irwin because I am restless and adventurous and wanted to wrestle a crocodile like him, and I later added Spinoza because I worship his pantheistic philosophy and look forward to returning to the earth's elements. My full name now is Albert Link Zamperini Irwin Spinoza Lawrence, but most just call me Link. When I was on the street they called me Scrappy; later, my wife called me "Link the Loser," and my disrespectful children called me "Stinky." On my future island, my name is Ikaika Kala Hana (ikeika-kaa-leh-aa), which means "strong, brave, and happy" in Polynesian, but everyone calls me "Kala" because that is what my friend Lilo called me.

So, this is my story.

Chapter 2

.

Pacific

There was nobody to say goodbye to, so I cleaned out what little money I had at the bank, collected my meager possessions, and drove my struggling Volkswagen to the small port city of Astor. I left my car on the street, walked to the nearest marina, and immediately saw a partially submerged sailboat. I asked the marina manager if it was for sale, and, startled, he said I could have it if I could get it out of there. To make a long story short, I managed to raise the boat, drag it to an isolated beach, and repair the hull.

I learned later it was a small, popular 25-foot Catalina Sport sailboat. It had a mainsail and jib, a small cabin with a bunk bed, a galley with a refrigerator, and a head. It also had a three-cylinder Yanmar inboard engine that surprisingly worked when it dried out, a generator, and a confusing array of electronic and navigation systems, but no radio. Fortunately, it also had a book on how to sail and three operator's manuals. After a week of repairing the boat, reading the book and manuals, and using the last of my money to buy provisions, I slowly motored out of the harbor into the vast blue Pacific Ocean. I did not know where I was going other than west.

I was exhilarated beyond imagination with the feeling of freedom. I felt like a prisoner who had just escaped his cell, narrowly evaded his captors, and was now safely on his way. I was glad to have escaped my dreadful life, my uncaring and disapproving parents, my mean-spirited wife Freya and the unappreciative children, and my disgusting job. I felt liberated from having to navigate the degrading, stratified social maze created by dead people, and strange extreme ideas that emerge when too many humans congregate in big cities detached from nature. I had escaped my cage and was flying to a new life of uncertainty, danger, and adventure. It was the beginning of my metamorphosis.

During the first few weeks, I was awed by the vast, open, and silent ocean. The days were filled with sun, water, and blue sky, the evenings with multi-colored sunsets, and the jet-black nights with thousands of brilliant white stars. The ocean was refreshing, humbling, indifferent, and beckoning. It overwhelmed me. Sometimes the isolation would cause bouts of loneliness, which would always make me remember one of my favorite authors, Louis Zamperini. He was my hero because he had survived many days alone on a raft adrift on the ocean during World War II. He survived by formulating a few rules to live by, such as the importance of staying active, the need to have hope, and why we must learn to adapt, which I had read in his book, *Never Give Up, Never Give In,* in my youth.

I took up my new way of life as a sailor with enthusiasm. I was surprised I enjoyed learning new things. My first priority was the need for fresh water, so I studied the desalinization manual carefully and gradually learned how to turn salt water into fresh. Even though I had bought a month's supply of foodstuffs, I decided to learn how to fish. There was no information on how to fish but I found a tackle box, tied a line to a lure that looked like a small fish, and dropped it in the water. It was just a few minutes when, to my surprise, the line was screaming out of my bloody hands; I went into a violent tug of war and eventually landed a twenty-pound tuna. My food problem was solved.

My next lesson was how to sail. I found the process of harnessing the invisible energy of the wind into physical momentum mysterious—it was like a Platonic form materializing. I quickly learned the basics, like tack and jibe, and nautical terms, like port and starboard. Learning to run and maintain the Yanmar engine was challenging, but nothing like the electronic system Loran-C, which I never completely figured out.

It had been a couple of weeks, and at four knots I figured I was somewhere in the deep South Pacific, probably around 20 degrees latitude and 140 degrees longitude. The weather had been relatively calm until one day all went dead still—I guessed this was a calm before the storm. Sure enough, within a few minutes, the sky went from blue to gray, and eventually was swirling with angry, black clouds. The wind steadily increased to around 60 to 70 knots, the waves became mountains, and my poor little Catalina began getting tossed around like a cork in class-5 rapids. It was a full-blown typhoon and I was sure I was going to die. I thought to myself, *fuck, I'm going to die, but still it's better than the sanitary engineer job.* I struggled to inflate the small life raft, strap on a life jacket, and abandon ship as it sank in the whipping winds. I held on to the raft for dear life for the next five hours, and to my surprise, I was still alive when the storm abated, the ocean calmed, and the sun reappeared.

I drifted for a few days with no water or food when a small, decrepit, rust-covered freighter appeared. I was elated to see it but confused because it eerily maintained its distance for some time, surveying me. I learned later the captain and crew were debating whether to save me because they were smuggling illegal contraband along with other cargo. Thankfully, their humanitarian instincts prevailed, they pulled alongside, and took me aboard.

The captain and eight crew members were a motley, disheveled, ragged, unshaven, taciturn, ignorant and smelly bunch. They treated me like I was a spy—distantly cool and wary. It was a sinister environment and I expected to be tossed overboard anytime. One time, I quietly snooped around the cargo hold, and was surprised at the odd variety of cargo-building materials, live animals, books, seeds and plants, musical instruments, machinery, and bags of white powder. I was in constant danger, but glad to be alive.

Chapter 3

Shipwreck

After about five days on the freighter, I was woken up by a loud commotion—mostly shouting and running—early in the morning. I quickly dressed, went up on deck, and saw the captain and crew in panic, scrambling aboard the few life boats and casting off. I grabbed one sailor just before he climbed over the railing and demanded he tell me what was going on! Terrified, he screamed they had been detected by a Polynesian naval vessel, that they hang drug smugglers, and that I should leave immediately because they had opened some cargo holds cocks to sink the ship and destroy the evidence.

Sure enough, the ship was beginning to seriously list to one side, so because it looked like all lifeboats were gone, I ran to the bridge to try and somehow salvage the ship. I wanted to steer it to a place where it could be grounded. After desperately learning some controls, I saw an island in the distance, cranked the wheel, aimed the ship straight at it, applied full throttle, and did my best to stay the course. The water was near the gunwales and the ship was almost swamped when I ran it aground at full speed on the island's shallow reef—I had made it, but just barely.

The pounding waves were pummeling the ship so violently, I thought it could break up at any time. I felt a deep foreboding because I was sure I would drown in the surf. In spite of my fear, I thought about the animals, so I stumbled through the shaking ship to their cargo hold, which fortunately had not been flooded, and quickly opened the cages. It was pandemonium when the panic-stricken animals were freed—cows, chickens, pigs, sheep and a dog. I led them to the deck where each was on their own to reach the beach. I jumped in the water, which was up to my chest, and an undertow immediately pulled me down and dragged me over some coral. Bloodied, I swam to the beach and pulled myself to its crest. It was late morning, the sun was strong, and I was utterly exhausted. I fell asleep under some palm trees.

I woke up in the evening shivering with the cold and wet, so I burrowed under some palm leaves and fell back to sleep. After a miserably cold night, I was elated to see the sun rise in the morning. It had been quite an ordeal, but I could not help thinking again that it was better than cleaning toilets.

It was then that I realized I had to learn how to survive, so I set out to explore the island for water, food, clothing, and shelter. It was a beautiful, large, tropical island with pristine, white, sandy beaches, palm trees, and a rugged interior. The weather was warm, although uncomfortably cold at night, and mildly humid with a warm, gentle breeze. The blue water was crystalline. I discovered an inlet and followed it to its source, a fresh water spring. I quenched my thirst and thought to myself, one problem solved.

I was surprised at the variety of animals on the island. There were exotic birds and turtles, along with the cows, chickens, pigs, and sheep that had survived the shipwreck with me. Late in the day I was resting on some high ground when I saw in the distance two fearsome-looking Bengal tigers. I kept very still, and fortunately, they did not see me. (If they had, I would not be writing this!) I suddenly realized I was in great danger and needed a weapon, but curiously, the danger excited me and made me feel alive. It felt good being in nature, on my own, close to the wild tigers and away from the domesticated city scavenger wolves feeding on their fellow wolves' carcasses.

As I was returning to my bed of palms, I heard a rustling in the grass that I thought might be a tiger, so I braced myself. Shortly, the very handsome golden retriever that had been on the ship with me emerged smiling, so I patted him and he began to lick my face. I laughed and thought he looked like George Burns of the television show Burns and Allen, so I called him George. Over time, George and I became inseparable friends—he followed me everywhere. I learned later that he was also a loyal and courageous soul.

The next morning, I went to the ship because I was hungry and cold, and I wanted to see what I could use. I struggled out through the surf, climbed aboard, and found my way to two unflooded cargo holds, one of which had some canned food and clothing, which I had collected. I saw various things I could use, like rope, canvas, tools, and some building materials. I decided I would come back the next day to salvage as much as I could. On my way out, I climbed to the bridge where I saw a chart of the area with the ship's last position plotted. I studied it and learned we were near the latitude and longitude I suspected in the Archipelago de Polynesia. I swam to the beach and headed back to my now bed-burrow in the sand.

I took a different return route and found myself at the edge of a clearing where I was startled to see seven or eight dark-skinned Polynesian men chanting and dancing around a stone statue, which I later learned was a Tiki religious icon or half-man/half-beast. They looked like warriors with their spears and elaborate headdresses, performing some religious ceremony. I crouched down, put my hand on George to quiet him, and watched them for some time. Suddenly, I became aware that one of them was looking at me. His stare was intense and I did not know whether to run or stay, so we just stared at each other for a long time. He was a fearsome, handsome, and intelligent-looking man in his forties. He looked like he could be their chief. I can't explain why, but I thought he looked like he wanted me to slip away quietly—probably for my safety. I took his hint and did just that. On my way back to my burrow, I felt lucky to have avoided them, and wondered where they came from. I climbed into my bed of palms and quickly fell asleep.

In hindsight, as strange as this may sound, I felt grateful for my unusual adventure. If I had not left the city, my life would have been more of the same awful, enervating experience in society, cleaning toilets until I died. But I *did* leave the city, and I was now living an alternate life that was exciting, adventurous, and energizing. Life was good.

Chapter 4

Salvage

The next day, George and I went back to the slowly disintegrating ship, taking care to avoid Polynesian warriors and Bengal tigers. Because the ship looked like it could break up at any time, I decided to try and salvage as much as I could. It turned out to be an arduous, three-day job. We struggled again through the surf, climbed aboard, and took a partially flooded stairway to the two dry cargo holds. To our surprise, we immediately heard a dog barking, which animated George, who quickly ran to the source. It turned out to be an absolutely gorgeous, young female golden retriever that we had overlooked. She looked much like George, with the same beautiful, thick golden-red fur and a comely countenance, except smaller. George was giddy with excitement as I freed her. He tried to nuzzle her, but she was having none of it. She was rather peeved, it seems, that we had left her behind. She gave George the cold shoulder that both disconcerted and irritated him.

George became rather quiet, withdrawn, and avoided her as much as possible. As it turned out, however, she was infatuated with George and, over time, began flirting and nuzzling him. He didn't stand a chance, and, as you will see, they became inseparable over time. It was only natural, of course, to call her Gracie from, the famous television show, *Burns and Allen*, starring George Burns and Gracie Allen.

I was anxious to find a weapon, so I started searching the hold. I had hoped to find a gun, but at least I managed to find a very sharp, high-quality, stainless steel Bowie knife and machete. I carried these everywhere, and, as you shall see, I used them often. Nearby, I happened to stumble across a long, leather case. I opened it and found a high-quality Quad Ultrarest compound bow, about 20 arrows, and a book on archery. With these weapons, I felt I could defend myself, especially after I studied archery. After months of practice, I became quite proficient and could usually hit a watermelon-sized object at fifty feet consistently.

I kept looking around and came across some canvas and rope that I thought would make a good temporary shelter. I also found vast amounts of building materials, including lumber, nails, and some fencing, along with tools like a hammer and screwdriver. I was concerned about food, so you can imagine how happy I was when I found seeds for corn, rice, and potatoes, as well as orange, apple, and pear tree saplings. In the other cargo hold, I found cloth, some utensils, flint, and a large metal cooking pot.

I also found a few things I did not know what to do with. I thought the red stove could be useful, the bagpipes could be fun to learn, the trove of books could be interesting to read, even though I was not an avid reader, and a long, rolled piece of thin metal might come in handy somewhere. I threw the drugs overboard because I did not want to be caught with them.

I began to wonder how I was going to get all this stuff to the beach, so I searched the ship for ideas. On the deck was a lifeboat that the crew had not taken, so I lowered it into the water and spent the next three days loading it with my haul, muscling it to the shore and up the beach. The heavy stove and books were the hardest to transport because they made the lifeboat unstable. As for the lumber, I just threw it all overboard and let the surf bring it to the shore where I collected it later. I used logs, rope, and a pulley from the ship to move the heavier items to higher ground. I had been thinking about a more permanent place to live and discovered a very large, full-canopied tree overlooking the ocean. I decided to move the trove there and cover it with a tarp.

After days of strenuous effort, it felt good to lie on the beach under the shady palm trees with George and Gracie, listening to the lapping waves and feeling the warm, tropical breeze. For the first time in my life, I felt supremely relaxed.

With my newfound leisure time, I found myself thinking more. I started pondering who I was, what I was doing there, and if we die, why does anything matter? I thought about my previous life and pondered the reasons it had been so bad: being born to the lower class, in an unstable family, sorely lacking an education. At the time, I did not know how bad my lot was and I had no idea how to escape it. It made me think of all the poor people back in Probatis in similar circumstances who silently suffer in the lower castes of society. I also thought about why I had been so unhappy and decided that desire, or wanting something I did not have, which was a lot of things, had been one source of my unhappiness. It occurred to me that I really did not need much to be supremely content. I felt my mind slowly coming alive in nature, where there was no advertising, with curiosity about everything, which made me think of the books I had salvaged. So, I went and got one, *The Death of Ivan Ilyich* by Leo Tolstoy, and started reading. I had no idea who Tolstoy was, but reading a man's thoughts as he was dying caught my interest. It was a good thing one of the books was a dictionary because it contained a number of words that were new to me.

I was changing. Somehow the island, isolation and nature were creating within me something different. Unlike my past, my existence was becoming more interesting, and I was excited to be alive.

Chapter 5

Isle de Belle

So many new experiences! Drifting on the open ocean, being shipwrecked, living with savages and tigers. These dangers were frightening, to be sure, but ironically, they also energized and enlivened me. It was as if I were waking up from a long, deep comatose sleep to a new, alive and vibrant world. I was scared to death but excited about it nevertheless.

I improved my palm bed with a stick-roof frame, grass bedding, and palm-leaf shingles, but I was still getting wet when it rained and I would shiver endlessly on frigid nights. It occurred to me that I might be on the island for a long time, so I decided to improve it further. I fashioned a simple wood frame over my bed with some lumber, lashed it together with rope, covered it with tarps, and threw in some blankets from the ship. On very cold nights I would start a warm fire at the entrance using the flint to keep me warm. It was primitive, but better than the wet and the cold of the first shelter.

I decided to explore the island in more detail, again avoiding tigers and savages. It turned out to be much larger than I'd originally thought, and numerous other islands were close by. It was a true archipelago. The interior was a dense jungle with wild roaring creeks and water falls. There were soft, balmy breezes near the ocean which gradually became hot and humid as I hiked inland.

I was concerned that my canned foods from the ship would run out soon, so I was relieved to discover the abundance of food. From the ocean were fish, crabs and clams, and on the island I saw bananas, coconuts, tubers, fruit, sweet potatoes and taro. I found the fresh water inlet and again followed it to its source. This time I thought about how this non-salty fresh water source could be piped through bamboo pipes to my living area.

When I returned to my small hut I lay on the grassy knoll overlooking the vast ocean, ate some sweet potatoes and fruit I had collected, and admired the spectacular pink and blue sunset. In spite of its challenges, I thought if one were to live far from civilization, in the state of nature, this island would be ideal. I decided to call it Ile de Bell, or beautiful island.

The next day I continued exploring. I was surprised at the variety of animals. I walked along the beach and saw fish, turtles and a shark. Further inland, I saw fire ants, snakes, and lizards. They all seemed harmless until George started barking wildly and this wicked-looking Kimono Dragon burst out of the undergrowth, bit Gracie and shook her, then aggressively charged me. I was surprised how fast and agile it was and was intimidated by its crocodile-like teeth. Its eyes had that dead reptile look. I started slashing it with my machete which only seemed to make it madder and fiercer. It tore the flesh on one of my legs and bit George, who had buried his teeth in its neck. I was surprised at my lack of fighting skill and decided I had to go all out to survive, so I lunged at the dragon, buried my knife in its head, and started violently slashing it with my machete while Gracie was busy chewing on one of its legs. Apparently, the dragon had enough because it abruptly backed off and ran away. It had been quite a fight; George, Gracie, and I were cut and bleeding but alive. We all recovered from our wounds and I started practicing my fighting skills.

That evening I was deep in thought, which had never happened in civilization. Despite the challenges, I thought how much I was enjoying life—a rare thought for me. In particular I thought about how much I was enjoying living in nature and reading. I had finished Tolstoy's *The Death of Ivan Ilyich* and was impressed with his views on happiness, especially why civilization-induced desires for money and prestige were not sources of happiness. Rather, true happiness comes from people. The next day I went to my book stash and picked out some philosophy books to read. I randomly chose Epictetus' *Discourses*, Plato's *Republic*, Boethius' *The Consolation of Philosophy*, and Ralph Waldo Emerson's *Self-Reliance*.

My body was relaxed and my mind was slowly awakening.

Chapter 6

Survival

Earlier I explored the island for food, water and clothing in order to survive. I now realized my survival depended on more—I needed to develop self-reliance. I had to rely on myself to figure ways to survive—my island had no grocery stores. I was reading early American philosopher Ralph Waldo Emerson's piece on self-reliance and learned how the unique early American rugged, industrious, individuals were the epitome of how to survive through self-reliance. It occurred to me this mind-set is quite the opposite in densely populated centers of civilization, like Probatis, where people come to rely on others for their survival. They somehow develop the view that it is others' obligation to care for them. They become totally reliant. It was obvious to me that most modern Utopianus city-dwellers would quickly die in nature.

It also occurred to me that in society, I had learned many things that were unnecessary and unproductive, mostly from ignorant or prejudiced teachers who have nothing to do with survival, whereas in nature, the teacher was a necessity. My social education had taught me how to navigate societies' systems, whereas necessity had taught me what to think and how to act in order to survive. My former teachers were too often political-ideological programmers, whereas necessity was nakedly based on reality and how to successfully navigate it.

Pondering what to think and do in order to survive made me recall Louis Zamperini's advice in his book, *Don't Give Up, Don't Give In.* He wrote that you must be persistent and never give up. It is important to commit to a goal and stay with it, because if your actions are aimless, like a ship with no rudder, you never go anywhere or achieve anything. He wrote that we must accept things and then move on, to challenge ourselves intelligently, to think in advance, and to always be prepared. Over time, I learned that a strong will brings action that enhances survival. I also learned to use my imagination to solve ostensibly insurmountable problems. Necessity was a good teacher that caused me to develop some critical skills like farming, husbandry, and carpentry. I put each of these skills to work when I designed, built and planted a garden under the large tree next to the ship salvage, that, in addition to the native foods, produced vegetables, potatoes and fruits; when I started building animal housing and filling it with many animals, chickens first; and finally when I designed and started building the treehouse, perhaps my most satisfying project. Fresh water, and how to get it to the treehouse, and new clothing were two challenges I had already figured out. One article of clothing I found difficult to replace was shoes.

Seeing savages and tigers, and the memory of the Kimono Dragon fight fresh in my mind, I started to practice with my knife and machete. I set up a dummy, a sack of dry grass, and stabbed it with my knife in various ways, and practiced slashing it with the machete. The dummy did not last long. The bow and arrow was the most important weapon to practice. I started reading the book on archery and practiced hitting different-sized targets at various distances. I learned the parts of the compound bow like the cam, cables, sight, and limbs, practiced my form, including aligning my body straight toward the target, learned about the draw and anchor point which was around my mouth, to keep my grip arm straight, and adopted the command-style method of archery, also called punching the trigger, where you shoot as soon as the pin passes over the target center, and finally learned about stance, nocking, bow draw, and anchoring. Nocking, by the way, means fitting and holding the arrow's notch to the bowstring. It was quite a fun learning experience, and it felt good to excel at something I had worked hard to achieve. Over time, I became quite proficient with all weapons, particularly the bow and arrow, with which, as I mentioned earlier, I could hit a watermelon-sized object at fifty feet.

I was enjoying learning so much, and due to my Scottish heritage, I decided my next project was to try and play the bagpipes I had salvaged from the ship. Initially, I was discouraged because the first sentence in the tutorial booklet was a quote from a certain Neil Monroe who wrote *To Make a Piper Go Seven Years*. Good grief! Would it really take me seven years to learn!? But I was determined. It started very slowly, learning the fingering, blowing constantly in the bag, and memorizing the tunes. I came to love the high-pitched skirl and powerful deep drones. Apparently, I made quite an impression on the island because scared animals would scurry away when I hit high A. The tigers disappeared for a while, and the savages were initially terrified—I learned later they began calling me Wa Hole, or the loud white man who strangles geese. It took time, but eventually I got where I could play a few tunes. My favorites were *Scotland the Brave, My Lodgings on the Cold, Cold Ground, Amazing Grace* and *The Green Hills of Tyrol*. Later, I learned *Sir Marcus Huntley's Highland Fling*.

It was late in the day and I had just finished working in the budding garden when I first met Lilo. I was sitting by the big tree when the fierce-looking savage I had seen earlier slowly approached me. Instinctively, I grabbed my machete and stood ready to fight. The savage stopped about twenty feet away and asked, in surprisingly good English, who I was and where I came from. His non-threatening—even *inviting* tone—disarmed me, so I put my machete down, said my name is Link Lawrence, that I was from a large country far way over the sea called Utopianus, and that my ship was sinking, so I beached it on this island. The savage said he had seen the ship, and then asked what I planned to do. I said I was not sure, but for now, I was just trying to survive. He smiled and said, "Join the club. His frank almost warm way of talking put me at ease. I asked him who he was, where he was from, and how he knew English. He said his name was Lilo and he was a tahu'a, or man of religion, in a tribe from another nearby island. He said many years ago he had been captured by some Englishmen and made to work on a military base where he learned to speak and read English. Eventually, he said he escaped and made his way home.

I was surprised at how much I was enjoying my interesting and lively conversation with Lilo. With a look of curiosity, he next asked me if I was married, and I said I was once but not now because my wife cheated on me. Lilo asked what *cheated* meant, and I said she had sex with another man, which surprised him. He said casual, promiscuous sex is encouraged in his society. He said he has a lovely wife who sleeps with many men, which makes many happy men and women in his village. He also said he had five busy, rebellious children, none of whom looked like him. We talked till the sun went down.

Later, Lilo asked me why I play a musical instrument that sounds like a cat being sodomized. I laughed and said the great highland bagpipes were invented by the Scottish people to intimidate and scare their enemies in war. Lilo said it did not surprise him because when he first heard them, he thought an angry god was about to smite him and that they were obviously more effective than banging coconut shells together. By that time, Lilo and I were sitting comfortably next to each other under the big tree overlooking the vast ocean.

He then said, "I hope you don't mind my asking you so many questions, but I find you fascinating." I said I was enjoying the conversation and he asked me about my books. He said he always sees me reading them. I said they are the valuable repository of my Western civilization's collective knowledge. I read about history, philosophy, religion, science, and biographies, to name a few. Lilo asked me what philosophy and psychology were and I said the pursuit of truth through reason and the nature of human behavior. Lilo looked puzzled and said his religion explained all that. I asked if his religion explained the internal combustion engine that propels cars, how planes' wings lift, and how large ships move over the water. Lilo said he had seen my large, beached ship and wondered how I could row such a large boat. He then asked me what a car was, and I said I was tired from working all day, and it was getting late, so we needed to continue our talk later. Lilo thanked me for the conversation. After he left, I pondered him. I thought his fierce looks were misleading. Rather, I found him funny, smart, curious, and worldly in some ways. He seemed like a new kind of human, unlike those back in Probatis. He had been warm, open, and friendly, and not hostile, guarded, and rude like many back home. He was a simpler and more natural kind of person, or the kind of person I thought we would naturally be outside of civilization. I liked him and hoped to see him again.

While George and Gracie were romping around, I spent some time thinking about the books I had read. I wondered if Epictetus' advocating suicide was right, whether knowledge was recollection as Plato claimed, how Emerson's emphasis on self-reliance had helped me survive, and how philosophy consoles when facing fearful situations, like when you are about to be executed, as Boethius so eloquently described. I had become a reader; I began aspiring to be a philosopher and began dreaming of a tree-house library for my books with a comfortable place to read.

Fortune was beginning to smile at me. My accomplishments brought success and self-respect, which in turn brought confidence and self-esteem. After the hectic beginning, my living environment on the island became slower, easier, and more peaceful. Perhaps above all, my increasing leisure time allowed me to pursue an emerging passion—the acquisition of knowledge through reading. Unlike my dreadful past life in Probatis, my future was bright and welcoming. I was looking forward to living it.

Chapter 7

Savages Attack

Unbeknownst to me, my peaceful life on Isle de Belle was about to come to an abrupt end. I continued to plant and expand my garden under the tree. It was beginning to produce potatoes and tomatoes, but it was going to be some time before the saplings produced apples and oranges. Because animals were eating my garden produce, I built a six-foot fence around it. Digging holes for the 4x4 posts from the ship was hard work, but connecting them with heavy-gauge wire mesh was easier.

This was the first time in my life that I experienced solitude. It is profound to be totally alone with yourself, except an occasionally solitary savage. I had never experienced solitude in the city with never-ceasing sirens, airplanes, and so many people. I found myself enjoying solitude, but I came to learn there are different kinds.

At first, I was lonely and found myself slipping into listlessness and empty contentment. I was not used to being alone. But over time I came to find solitude energizing and soothing. The profound silence of nature was healing. Somehow, being alone with my uncontaminated thoughts brought me meaning and purpose because I started thinking about things important to me, establishing goals, and making plans on how to achieve them. I thought about expanding my garden and working on the treehouse. This brought me happiness, but being a social animal, I still longed for human contact. George and Gracie were comforting, but they were dogs, so I decided to further my relationship with Lilo and explore the island to see if there were any other humans.

I was enjoying my books so much that, at random, I started reading Spinoza's *Ethics* and Frank Bourne's *The History of the Romans* because I wanted to know about ancient history. Then, for the fun of it, I started reading two poems: Robert Frost's *The Road Not Taken* and Walt Whitman's *O Captain! My Captain!* I also kept working on the bagpipes. It seemed to me the animals were getting used to the skirl because I was getting an audience when I played. I think their favorite tune was *Amazing Grace*, but they got really excited when I played *Scotland the Brave*—the pigs would snort, the dogs would howl, and the chickens would crow.

It was when I was working on the bamboo piping from the spring that a panicked-looking Lilo appeared and said that I was in mortal danger. He said at first, they were amazed, awed, and terrified of your pipes, but they have changed. He said they now think my pipe's squeal is an angry god because their spiritual home has been desecrated and the sacred burial grounds defiled. Terrified, Lilo said the chief of the tribe, Lucius, is a mean-spirited, cruel leader who intends to kill me. Quickly, he said I had to run and hide, and with that, he suddenly disappeared into the jungle.

As soon as Lilo left, George and Gracie began barking wildly, and nine to ten fearsome-looking, war-painted savages burst from the undergrowth armed with spears and long knives led by their angry, evil-looking chief Lucius. It was the beginning of a fearsome running fight for my life. I turned and ran as fast as I could, hoping to get lost in the dense vegetation. My heart was pounding when I dove into a clump of ferns and grass to hide. I stayed as still and quiet as I could while the savages beat the brush around me. They were so close I could hear them breathing when suddenly one yelled, and a spear was thrust into my clump, narrowly missing me. Apparently, the savages could smell me, so hiding was a waste of time. I flew out and stabbed one with my knife, which startled them and again ran for my life with them in hot pursuit. It was a close chase as I flew through the jungle.

After running and dodging spears for 100 yards, I stopped abruptly, spun around, and began firing arrows into their midst. I dropped three of them, which momentarily surprised them. The remaining six quickly regained their courage and sent a barrage of spears at me, slicing one leg and grazing an arm, both of which began to bleed. I again turned and ran with them on my heels.

I wasn't outrunning them, so I again stopped and sent more arrows at them, dropping one. The others charged, and a fearsome hand-to-hand fight ensued between my machete and knife and their long knives. It was a good thing I had practiced—I was surprised how deft I was with my weapons. I was holding my own. Unfortunately, I was outnumbered when two of them grabbed my arms, and a third thrust his knife at my stomach, which narrowly missed because I rolled at the last second, and the savage holding one of my arms was stabbed. I fell to the ground and wildly swung my machete and cut off one savage's foot and another's arm, and then took off running again as if my life depended on it—which it did.

After running another fifty yards they were slowly gaining on me, so I decided, thinking a good offense would be my best defense, to turn and fight it out with the remaining three. It was a brief, intense fight with knives and fists. I thought I was a goner when suddenly George and Gracie, who had chased a savage back to his canoe, burst out of the undergrowth and started mauling the savages from behind. This distracted them long enough for me to punch one on the side of the head as hard as I could, sending him lifeless to the ground. With that, the remaining two, which included Lucius, ran away. It had been one hell of a good fight, one I would have paid to watch, and I was glad to be alive.

I hobbled back to my tent and spent the next couple of days healing and pondering whether human nature was good or evil. I thought about the difference between Lilo and Lucius. Lilo is gentle and friendly whereas Lucius is vicious—he wanted to kill me even though I had never wronged him. I wondered what makes people like Lucius evil, and it occurred to me it was ignorance. Lucius and his followers were superstitious, a consequence of ignorance, but then Lilo was also religious. I wondered if it was nature and civilization that made good and evil people.

I also thought about morality and whether good and evil depended on circumstance. Could Lucius' evil nature be derived from the need to be aggressive to survive in nature? In some respects, I thought his evil traits may really be good traits. I recalled something I had read in one of the philosophy books from the ancient philosopher Protagoras—that man is the measure of all things. My brain was so overwhelmed with thoughts that I hit the pause button, decided to pursue these thoughts later, and went to sleep.

As I was drifting off, I thought that, in spite of my challenges, my life was much better on Isle de Belle than back in Probatis. I recalled my awful wife, Freya, my smelly port-a-potty job, and others' disrespect. I thought how good my life is and of the treehouse, and a feeling of comfort and joy lulled me to sleep.

Chapter 8

Treehouse

The bloody fight with savages and occasional hungry tigers made me realize I needed to build a safer home. Because my tent home had blown away a couple of times in high winds, I decided my new home should be more substantial. It was also a good time to start building because the last savages had left in their canoe and I had salvaged a lot of tools and building material.

I thought about building inland in a meadow I had seen, on the edge of the beach, or even a floating home in the lagoon. I was pondering this while sitting under the tree in the garden amongst the plants and animals when I looked up and was struck by the idea of building a treehouse. I got up and walked around the huge, magnificent tree, studying it carefully. It had large, mature limbs that could support a treehouse; the lowest limbs were high enough to be beyond leaping tigers and savages; it was close to the beach and had a sweeping view of the ocean. Also, I had already started a garden under it, which was thriving due to the fertile soil. It was close to the freshwater spring, and it had a full, dense canopy that would protect it from the intense, tropical sun.

I thought about what it should look like. I considered having part of it on the ground or one very large house in the tree. The more I studied the tree, the more I realized it could hold multiple structures, so I began envisioning a main building, a living room, a bedroom, and a restroom, all connected by skywalks made of ropes and planks. I imagined piping water to the house from the spring, having a shower in the bathroom, raising food in the enclosed garden, and installing torch lights throughout for light at night.

I started by designing the main building. I wanted it to be comfortable, warm, inviting and safe. I envisioned a central fire pit for warmth, which made me think of the red stove that would make a good fireplace, comfortable sofas with thick cushions, a kitchen with sinks and running water, storage for food, a mouth-watering pot of stew, and a covered porch. I saw the limb that the living room would be built on because it was stout and safely high. I also decided to build my treehouse in increments, starting with the living room. Excitedly, I grabbed some paper and a pencil and began sketching the layout and construction of the structure. I could not believe how wonderful it would be when I was done. I was so pleased with my drawing, I could not wait to live in it, and started work the next morning after a sleepless night.

I had decided I wanted to build quality, permanent structures, so I proceeded slowly and deliberately. The first thing I did was gather my tools, including a saw, a hammer, a measuring tape, an auger and a level, and then looked at my building materials. Fortunately, I had salvaged a lot of material from the ship, including lumber, nails, screws and lags.

Building the foundation was the hardest of all jobs. I found some stout Kapok trees and laboriously cut them down and hewed notches so they would fit snugly in the tree bows. Hoisting these heavy timbers with block and tackle and attaching them to the limbs with lags was strenuous. I also extended the beams for a porch and gradually decked the surfaces. It was hard work, but I had an important and meaningful goal which kept reminding me of Louis Zamperini's advice to persevere. Eventually, I had a large level solid platform on which to start building the living room.

My unfinished sketch of the living room

I had not anticipated the dangers of the project. First, I was working 30 to 50 feet in the air, and if I slipped and fell, I would probably die. Indeed, one time when I was working on the siding, I slipped and started to fall head first. I was saved only by a limb below that I grabbed for dear life. After that, I tied a safety rope around my waist.

Second, I had to constantly keep an eye out for hungry tigers. I could see them outside the fence, milling around, trying to get to the animals. This was particularly dangerous when I was on the ground working on something because I was usually engrossed in what I was doing and a tiger could easily creep up and ambush me from behind. I became fully aware of my surroundings and eventually grew eyes in the back of my head.

It was a good thing I was alert because I was attacked one time. It was hard to see the tiger because he had crouched down and blended almost seamlessly with the vegetation. I always wore my knife and carried my machete, but this time, I had set the machete and bow down about twenty feet away. Luckily, George barked at him just as he charged. Instinctively, I threw my knife at him, which made him pause just long enough to let me race to my bow, load an arrow, and fire just as he was about to pounce. It is a good thing I had practiced because the arrow went straight into his chest. He stopped, leaped, writhed, shrieked, growled, and ran away. It had been a short, violent encounter, and I was glad to be alive. From then on, I developed a special, fearful respect for these dangerous and powerful predators.

When the foundation was completed, I started thinking about access to the main building, which I began calling Halcyon because it was making me optimistic and happy. My main concern was safety, so I needed something to prevent animals and savages from getting in. I decided to build a platform about halfway up the tree with two retractable stairways with rigged ropes that could be raised and lowered.

I had salvaged a large roll of galvanized metal from the ship which I cut, formed, and wrapped around the tree trunk below the platform. This would prevent animals with claws and rodents from climbing the tree trunk. I spent my first night on the platform after raising the stairs and felt quite safe, unlike sleeping on the ground.

Because of the occasional tropical rain, I decided to build the roof next. I erected a frame of posts and beams from the foundation and started collecting broad leaf ferns which I wove tightly together with vines. The hardest part was keeping the roof from leaking where it was penetrated by tree branches. After many experiments, I heated some tar shingles from the ship and poured the hot liquid around the tree trunk. A couple of days later, the roof was deluged by a heavy rain, and the living room remained perfectly dry. I was quite pleased.

Next, I decided to start enclosing the living room. I built a solid railing about four feet high in the living area and an open-sided railing on the porch. I left the area above the railing open for the warm tropical breezes and spectacular vista. I was now ready to install the red fireplace/stove and chimney. It was heavy, but I managed to muscle it to the center of the living room and attach its stove pipe chimney. I ran into a problem because the hot stove pipe could catch the thatch roof on fire. I solved this by fashioning some stainless steel into a double-walled section that kept the hot pipe away from the roof. I also found a place for the stew pot next to the hot stove and began making thick, tasty stews using vegetables from the garden and an occasional chicken. The stew was always hot and filling.

My next project was the most enjoyable—furnishing the living room. I built a large kitchen desk with two sinks, a cabinet for food storage, some shelving, and drawers. I next built a large sofa and made cushions from fabric scraps for comfort. Finally, I fashioned two torches for light. When I was finished, it was a wonderfully warm, dry, safely high, and comfortable home. In the evenings, I would build a fire, light the torches, and sit on the couch eating heated stew while enjoying the spectacular evening sunsets over the ocean.

The living room of Halcyon was mostly done, so I began working on other projects. The first was to continue cultivating the garden and slowly increasing the height of the fence, because I noticed some tigers had come close to scaling it. I spent considerable time improving the animals' pens. The animals (cows, chickens, pigs, and sheep) seemed quite content. Occasionally, I would open a gate so they could forage outside their pens, but they rarely went far and always returned. George, Gracie and I closely watched them in case tigers appeared. They were a constant cacophony of happy grunts, moos and baahs. I was pleasantly surprised when they began bearing young.

I had always kept in mind the freshwater spring I'd discovered earlier. I decided to try to pipe it to my home, so I spent some time cutting bamboo and figuring out how to connect them. I started the pipeline at the spring and built about 1,000 feet of pipe to the treehouse. I planned to provide water for the animals, garden, kitchen sink, and future bathroom. I built a water trough for the animals, installed sprinklers for the garden, a capped bamboo with holes, installed a line to the kitchen sink, and stubbed a line to the future bathroom.

I had been so busy building halcyon, I had little time for other pursuits. I did take the failing lifeboat out a couple of times to fish and managed to do a little reading. I had been told that early Utopianus was an ideal place of freedom, wealth, and opportunity due to its founding documents, so I found among my books Utopianus' Constitution, Bill of Rights, and *Declaration of Independence* and started reading them. I was struck by concepts that I had no idea existed. They claimed humans are entitled to life, liberty and the pursuit of happiness; they described democratic representative government, and provided for negative rights like free speech, freedom of religion and assembly. I enjoyed my reading so much I decided to make my dream of a library come true. It would be comfortable with a big chair by a warm fire. I envisioned it as the ideal place to read.

While I was working on the piping, I was surprised to see Lilo below staring at halcyon. I immediately climbed down and greeted my friend. I was glad to see him. He first said he was sorry for his tribe's

Completed Halcyon

attack and was glad Kala was okay. He said many tribe members were angry with Lucius for inciting the attack and he may be deposed. Then, pointing to the treehouse, he asked *What is this?* I said it was my new home and he responded, *In a tree?* I said I'd give him a tour, and proceeded to show him the retractable access stairs, living room, fireplace, comfortable sofas, and porch. I then told him about my future plans for running water, a bathroom and shower. He started asking questions like how I cut some joints, where I got the building materials, if the fireplace worked, and where I got the plants and animals. He said he had never seen anything like it and was rendered speechless.

Lilo and I then went and sat on the living room sofas, I built a fire, and we began talking about my recent readings. I described *Utopianus' Constitution, The Bill of Rights,* and *The Declaration of Independence.* He was quite interested and said it was good that I was ruled by abstract ideas. He could see how they could make society safer and more just. We, on the other hand, are ruled by one man, the chief, with the help of his council. As a result, we must often follow capricious laws based on the chief's opinions. We also get an occasional evil chief, like Lucius, who makes our lives miserable. Lilo continued and said he also liked our emphasis on freedom and safety, or life and liberty. With these ideals, it appeared to him that we could travel most places freely. The tribes' overarching ethic is "might makes right," which puts us in perpetual wars. If we happen to stray into another tribe's territory, we are immediately attacked and often enslaved or killed. Lilo said we are prisoners in our own territory. With that, Lilo thanked me for the tour, said he enjoyed our conversation, and that the treehouse was amazing, but that he had to leave in order to catch the tides to his home island.

George and Gracie's relationship had come a long way since Gracie had given George the cold shoulder. They were always together playing, running, and swimming, so it was no surprise when Gracie got pregnant and gave birth to seven pups. Suddenly, we were overrun by a bunch of rambunctious goldens. They soon became a fiercely protective pack of dogs.

My life was getting better every day on Isle de Belle. I was accomplishing much, I had a purpose in life, I was enjoying successes, I was overcoming daunting problems with my ingenuity and skill, and I was creating a new, happy life. Because of this, unlike my past, I was gaining confidence, a sense of self-worth, and self-respect. On top of this, every evening, I would sit on my treehouse porch, listen to the breaking waves, feel the soft, warm tropical breeze, hear the wind rustle through the palms, and enjoy the jungle's sweet smells, while gazing at the ocean's spectacular multi-colored sunsets. It was a heavenly place, far from the city's oppressive traffic and sounds of sirens. I was, for all intents and purposes, in paradise.

Chapter 9

Dangerous Trek

Even though I was enjoying life on idyllic Isle de Belle, something was missing. I had finished the living room and started working on other projects. I decided to delay building the library and bedroom because I needed a bathroom. I picked a sturdy limb nearby and began constructing the foundation. After completing the siding and roof, I built a toilet, sink and shower. I found a sunny high limb and built a water-holding tank and extended the bamboo water piping to it and filled it with water. The sun heated the water, so I was giddy with excitement to get my first warm shower in months. I loved taking a shower in a largely open space, high in the air, in a warm tropical breeze.

I rigged a suspended-rope walkway with solid-plank flooring connecting the living room and restroom. It was a little scary because the walkway swayed, especially in a strong wind, but I steadied it with stays. I also continued to tend the garden, look after the animals, and gradually increase the fence height.

Even though I was busy, I always found time to read every day. This time it was Henry David Thoreau's *Walden* that I identified with because it was about living a simple, solitary life. I particularly liked Thoreau's advice to *simplify, simplify, simplify*. It made me realize how I used to yearn for things in society that I did not need. Indeed, living simply on Isle de Belle taught me human nature is easily satisfied.

The solitary life was nice, but I was getting lonely. I saw Lilo occasionally, but I missed human companionship, even though in Probatis, they had abused me. I don't know why, but I decided to take a long hike. I was interested in exploring, seeking adventure, and securing another food source. In hindsight, however, I think subconsciously, I really wanted to find other humans. It turned out to be quite a fortuitous and exciting trek.

I packed a little food and headed out with George on my heavily calloused feet. I followed the coastline because the interior was too dense and rugged. I was soon in unfamiliar country, traversing broad, white, sandy beaches, occasional dense jungle, rivulets, and waterfalls. The deep blue ocean was always on my left, tropical palm trees on my right, and a warm breeze in my face. I knew my island was big, but soon realized it was much bigger than I thought because there was no end to the coastline.

Wildlife was hard to see, but I felt constantly watched, including by an occasional tiger. George would sometimes charge into the jungle, barking wildly at something, and then come running back. I was ready with my machete in one hand and bow and arrow in the other, just in case. I found the uncertainty and danger thrilling.

Around dusk, we came to a place where the sandy beach widened. I was surprised to see some debris that had washed ashore. I went to get a closer look and saw some plastic bottles and a shoe, and then I was shocked to see some human footprints. I immediately crouched down and surveyed the entire beach. About 150 feet away, I made out a small dark mass. George and I cautiously walked toward it. I was gripping my knife and machete, preparing to fight if necessary. When we got within twenty feet, I was startled to see three young, terrified people huddled closely together.

It was a young woman, probably in her early twenties, a teenaged boy and girl, I guessed sixteen or seventeen. The young woman had a sharpened stick that she nervously pointed at my chest. George growled and I calmly said "Please don't stab me. I like my body the way it is." The unexpected humor seemed to put her at ease. I said "I don't know who you are, or if you speak English, but you are in great danger. I have seen tigers, and this is their hunting time. You are dangerously exposed." They were silent, except one of the teenagers began to whimper. I said, "You must trust me. Act quickly and do as I say if you want to survive." I told them to dig a hole in the sand just big enough for the four of us and deep enough so only our heads are exposed. They started digging with alacrity while I ran and collected some very sharp sticks and brambles. I dragged them back to our redoubt and started building an abatis, or a barbed outer barrier that would discourage the tigers. No sooner had we finished and awkwardly huddled together, two hungry- looking tigers began circling us. I wasted no time, loaded an arrow, drew my bow and nailed one in the neck. It leaped and howled and both quickly ran away.

The wary women seemed to relax somewhat and talked and patted George who was curled up in a corner. George loved the attention. I noticed that they looked hungry, so I offered them some of my food which they quickly ate. I was able to see them more clearly and was struck by the young woman's beauty. The female teen was rather homely and the male teen withdrawn and scrawny. The teenagers eventually fell asleep, I stayed awake, on guard, and the young woman dozed occasionally, but would awaken to keep me company.

We spent a dangerous night huddled together. Two or three times, tigers approached, but between the abatis and my arrows, they quickly ran off. I must say, in spite of the danger, the best part of the night was being pressed against soft female bodies, and especially breasts. I don't know what they were thinking, but it had been a long time since I had sex with a woman, and my sensuous instinct was stirred.

In the morning, I asked everyone if they wanted to go with me to my house. I said it was a long, dangerous hike, maybe ten miles, and there were some natural obstacles like roaring streams, and we could be attacked by tigers at any time. However, I told them, it was a safe place, and with that they enthusiastically agreed. I told them to stay close together, because the cats are always looking for strays. With that, we packed our meager belongings and started to hike.

It was a slow walk back, during which we were constantly being watched. I sent arrows into the rustling jungle a couple of times to keep the cats on the defensive. I was concerned about crossing a roaring stream because only one of us could shinny across the rope I had strung and I was concerned that those waiting to cross would be attacked. It was a tense crossing but we made it even though the young teen girl almost slipped and fell into the roaring water. Luckily, I grabbed her by the collar just as she began to fall.

It was a tremendous relief when Halcyon came into view. They were astounded that it was a treehouse and thrilled when Gracie met us at the gate with her brood of puppies. I opened the gate and let them spend some exciting time exploring the garden and animal pens while being mobbed by retriever puppies. I closed the gate, lowered the stairs, and led everyone up to the living room. They asked why there was a wide metal band around the tree and I said that it was to prevent leaping tigers and climbing animals. I was greatly relieved that we had made it and were now safe.

As they examined the living room, I lit a fire in the fireplace, lit the torches for light, and started a fire under the pot of stew I had made a few days earlier. I showed them the completed bathroom with a toilet, running water, and a hot shower, which astonished them. I then told them of my plans for a bedroom and showed them the location. We then went back to the living room where they curled up on the couches and, famished, devoured the hot stew. Eventually, everyone, feeling safe, full and warm, fell asleep. It had been a good day.

In the morning, I got up and started making coffee and heating the remaining stew. The young woman immediately got up and asked if she could take care of the kitchen and cooking. I was surprised because she had not talked to me much. I smiled and agreed, and went down to work in the garden and animal pens. Shortly, she brought me a cup of delicious, hot coffee.

I thanked her for the coffee. She then asked my name and why I was there. When I told her, she said that Link was an unusual name, and asked where it came from. When I told her it was from a video game my parents liked, she chuckled and said, "A video game?" I then asked what her name was and how she got there. She said Anabel, but most people call her Ann, and her friends, Annie. She said she was taking the two teenagers to a mission in Australia and, like me, their passenger ship had sunk, they had drifted in a lifeboat for many days and had just washed ashore when I found them.

Then the teenagers showed up, and said their names were Logan and Ella. They asked what I was doing so I described the garden and animals. Logan, who had grown up on a farm, took immediate interest in the garden. He identified all the plants, fruits and trees and asked if he could work in it. I handed him the hoe. Then Ella, who had wandered over to the animal pens and was busy getting to know them, said she also had grown up on a farm and loved animals. She asked if she could care for them, and again, I was more than happy to oblige. It was fortuitous, because within an hour, Ann took over the kitchen, Logan the garden, Ella the animals, and I was freed to finish the bathroom and work on the bedroom.

I was taken by Ann. Not only was she handsome, but also calm, graceful and cheerful. Over time, I also learned she was funny, resilient, and sensuous. She really liked sex. But for now, she was wary but obviously interested in me.

My life became different after the trek. I now had three other human companions, a pack of goldens, and I was no longer lonely. Life was good.

Chapter 10

Tigers

We all were enjoying the comfortable and safe living room while gradually getting to know each other. Evenings were spent sitting around the fire, cooking meals, listening to the sounds of the jungle, and enjoying the spectacular view. I found myself Tarzan-like, wearing fewer clothes because of the balmy weather, and always barefoot. I still had a large trove of materials from the ship, which had disintegrated long ago, along with the lifeboat I had salvaged.

I was surprised at how well Ann and the teenagers were managing Halcyon without me, so I quickly finished the bathroom and started work on the now much-needed second bedroom. I found a high, sturdy limb and began building a skywalk to it and laying a foundation. One time, Logan showed up and asked if he could help. Astounded, I readily agreed, and between the two of us, we hauled heavy foundation timbers to the limb and started on the flooring. I showed him how to use tools like the level, hammer, augur, chisel, and wrench. Because there were more of us, we needed to expand the garden to grow more food, so Logan, Ann, and I began building a new outer fence in some places, and Logan started preparing the soil and planting. We planned together, worked closely as a construction team, and laughed a lot. Ella often came over from the animal pens and helped. I found working with all of them most enjoyable.

Much to everyone's surprise, I continued my reading. Two books in particular made quite an impression. I was intrigued by Sigmund Freud's idea in *Civilization and Its Discontents* that humans are incapable of happiness because civilization represses their instincts. I wondered if it were true. I also found interesting John Bowman's *Aegean Summer*, in which he described his unhappiness working in a high-pressure job, living in a competitive, capitalistic society. Having once lived in civilization and now in nature, I found both author's poignant insights eerily true.

One evening, Ann saw me practicing the bagpipe chanter and asked if I knew how to play bagpipes. I said I was a beginner but had learned a few tunes. She smiled broadly and said she was Scottish and could dance the Highland fling. I immediately got my bagpipes, quickly tuned them, and, to Ann's obvious delight, started playing *Sir Marquis of Huntly's Highland Fling*. To my surprise, she then began athletically dancing the fling by leaping into the air with one hand on her hip and another in the air. The teens quickly joined in the fun, trying to imitate Ann. Later, I taught Logan to play the pipes, and Ann taught Ella the Highland fling.

My new companions, though, most enjoyed the bathroom, and, in particular, the high semi-open shower. We took turns taking hot showers and quickly got accustomed to nudity. I happened to see Ann a few times showering naked and was attracted to her pale white skin, large breasts, and flowing red hair. I think Ann liked being admired because after a time, she asked if I would call her Annie, which was an intimate gesture. At first, I was hesitant because of the ill-treatment I'd received from women in the past, but I had changed and was now confidently masculine. I started calling her Annie.

Getting to know the teens was difficult because they were not as open. I got to know Logan first because we were working on the treehouse and garden together, and I was teaching him archery. He was seventeen, scrawny, withdrawn, and he stuttered. Ella was harder because I was only with her when we were with the animals. She was sixteen, homely, insecure, skittish, and immature. She once said the most important thing in life is how you look. They were obviously interested in each other, but their relationship was awkward.

What I noticed was how Ella and Logan's human proclivities naturally emerged in nature. Logan excelled at carpentry and archery. He practiced archery endlessly and became quite good, and he got so skilled at carpentry, I let him work on the bedroom alone while I pondered a second bedroom and library. In contrast, Annie spent her time cooking in the kitchen, and Ella enjoyed nurturing the animals and their offspring. They were mostly interested in reproduction and children. I was reassured to see genders pursuing their natural instincts in nature, unlike the artificial societal induced roles my former teacher had tried to foist upon me. I enjoyed watching these young teens maturing naturally.

I wondered why they were maturing differently in nature, and then it occurred to me that they were freer in nature. Logan had less male competition, was not bullied, and no longer had to physically fight for respect. Ella was freed from stifling societal norms that pigeonholed her future, female backstabbing intrigue, and judgments about her appearance. Both were free of straitjacket societal roles and others' opinion "jails," and neither had to dissemble in order to successfully navigate societal norms. In nature, they shed their masks. Their lives were more independent and excitingly adventurous. Metaphorically, their transition from civilization to nature was like shedding clothes. In society, everyone wears layers of clothing that constrain, whereas, in nature, they wear little, if any, clothing, which liberates them. They were freed to become what they *were*, rather than what somebody else *thought* they should be.

It was a warm afternoon when I suggested we all go swimming in the crystal-clear lagoon. Everyone enthusiastically agreed, and Annie and Ella packed a lunch. Of course, everyone, as you would suspect by now, quickly shed all clothing and swam naked. It felt so natural and liberating.

A couple of days later, while Logan and I were working on the bedroom, Ella let out a blood-curdling scream, came running from the animal pens, and bounded up the stairs. Breathless, she stammered that she had seen a savage, so Logan and I grabbed our bows and went to investigate. There was rustling in the brush; we braced for a fight and out walked Lilo. To everyone's surprise, I went over, shook his hand, embraced him, and said "Good to see you!" I then introduced him to

Annie, Ella, and Logan, as my close friend, and explained that he was a tahu'a, or peaceful man of religion. Lilo said he was sorry for scaring Ella, who said she didn't know any savages. With that, we all went to the living room and talked while Annie and Ella made dinner. Lilo told them his life story and said many times how pleased he was to meet my friends. He told them it was good they came because, he said, "Link was getting lonely."

The retriever puppies were now about six months old and the size of small adults. They had become a rambunctious pack that loved to run, chase wildlife, and, above all, swim in the lagoon. Along with George and Gracie, as you will shortly see, they had also become a fiercely protective pack.

Savages had attacked me, I'd fought tigers and beat a Kimono dragon, but our next assault was the most ominous. It was late morning  on a warm, sunny day. The gate to the central compound was open, the animals were out everywhere, the golden retrievers were swimming, and everyone was doing their jobs. Annie and Ella cared for the animals, and Logan and I were working in the garden. I was alarmed when the sounds of the jungle and animals went silent, and I quickly realized how lax, unprepared, and vulnerable we were to a tiger attack. I told Logan to run for his bow and arrows while I grabbed my knife and machete. Suddenly, four large, fearsome-looking Bengal tigers charged out of the jungle.

Bengal tigers are awesome killing machines. These cats were well over ten feet long and 650 pounds of muscle. They had black and white stripes with blood-red-orange swaths and large, lethal, penetrating eyes. Their huge, white fangs and sharp claws could tear an animal apart in seconds. As they charged, their loud guttural growl was enough to paralyze any victim with fear.

They quickly and viciously attacked and killed a cow and two sheep, and bit Annie's leg as she tried to run. I attacked them with all I had, slashing one with my machete and burying my knife in another, which only seemed to make it angry. I was getting painfully clawed on my left arm when I saw one tiger mauling Ella's head. Tigers usually bite their victim's neck to collapse their trachea and suffocate them or violently shake their back to break their spine and paralyze them. This one was chewing on Ella's neck and head, which usually kills quickly. It was carnage with blood and body parts everywhere and animals whaling, humans groaning, and tigers mauling. I thought we did not have a chance and we would all die.

Suddenly, everything changed. Logan appeared on the landing and sent a withering fusillade of arrows into the cats; George, Gracie and their pack came roaring out of the undergrowth and started mercilessly biting the cats from all angles; then Lilo, with four of his warriors, burst from the jungle and sent a barrage of spears into the astonished cats. I was so encouraged by all this backup that I started swinging my machete with abandon, decapitating one cat. When the dust settled, they were all dead.

The tigers had killed two cows, three sheep, four pigs, a few chickens, and one golden. Annie's leg and my left arm were seriously lacerated and bleeding, requiring stiches. Ella's head wounds were by far the worst and we were not sure if she was going to live. Luckily, Lilo was not only a tahu'a, but also a medicine man who knew natural remedies for wounds. He stitched us up, gave us natural antibiotics, and primitive splints for broken bones. It took months for us to recuperate, during which time we bonded due to the traumatic shared experience. We were all glad to be alive.

Fortunately, Ella recovered from her wounds after a long convalescence. She said her mauling was a horrific experience. She said the tiger was very heavy and forced her head down as he chewed on the back of her scalp. She said she felt the tiger's hot breath on her neck as she heard the sound of cracking bones. I noticed the experience changed her and she became calmer and more mature. She later told me she now values life rather than appearance.

I came away with two revelations from the tiger attack. The first was that nature can be very dangerous. It occurred to me that I could die in nature from a wide variety of causes like dangerous animals, untreated diseases, and falling from a treehouse. Nature may look tranquil, but it can be brutal. The other revelation was how much I missed loving and being loved by a woman. Earlier I had thought something was missing in my life. I learned that my growing intimacy with Annie was satisfying a deep need. I was happily falling in love.

Chapter 11

Romance and Love

We all grew closer while recuperating and spent easy days together sunning on the beach, playing in the surf, swimming in the lagoon, and enjoying evening dinners, talking and laughing with a gentle warm breeze. It was wonderful being around partially clad, young, and often naked women swimming in the lagoon or taking a shower; it was so natural and energizing. Romance and love were in the air between Logan and Ella, me and Annie, and of course, the goldens. Halcyon was safe and comfortable and I was close to finishing the main bedroom; however, we could see that a second one would be needed soon. Even though we had killed four tigers, we continued to see an occasional one, usually around the animal pens, so we stayed alert.

I was so taken with philosophy that I decided to read some of the more profound philosophic books I had acquired. I read Aristotle's *Nicomachean Ethics* and pondered his Doctrine of the Mean, Marcus Aurelius' *Méditations* and Cicero's *Tusculan Disputation* and learned about Stoicism. By far the most complex and confusing book I read was

Kant's *Critique of Pure Reason.* I struggled to understand his idealistic philosophy but was struck one day with his insight that precepts without concepts are blind and concepts without precepts are empty. They say learning is a series of flights and perches, and now with Kant, I flew to a new perch.

One day, when I was deep into my reading, Annie appeared and asked where I got all the books. She said she was impressed that I was such a diligent reader and intellectual and started asking me many questions about what I learned. I told her some of my favorite insights were that we are what we think and Protagoras' mistaken view that man is the measure of all things. Over time, as we discussed the books, our relationship became deeper with an intellectual dimension.

It was so satisfying to watch the young people grow and flourish on Isle de Belle. Initially, all they talked about was going home to Scotland, but as time passed, they talked more about the island, their plans, and each other. Logan, who had been scrawny, withdrawn, clumsy, and mildly autistic, was now buff from hard work, engaging, skilled, and surprisingly savvy. He became quite reliable, and these traits were not imposed on him; rather, they evolved naturally and voluntarily. He was always whistling when working in his garden or building something. Ella's transformation was more striking. In addition to maturing, she had transformed from an ugly duckling to a beautiful swan. Her gorgeous, long blond hair, perfect pearl-white skin, and fully formed Rubenesque body were gorgeous. She also became loving and generous.

The two spent all their free time together talking, swimming and hiking. It was obvious they had fallen in love. Sure, they had their disappointments and fights, but they always made up quickly. Predictably, they also became more physical, kissing and hugging, and would be gone for hours, presumably to have sex. Their uninhibited sexual nature emerged naturally. It occurred to me that their desires and sexual impulses were innocently pure, unlike back in confusing and unnatural civilization where others' often wrong opinions and agendas, and oppressive societal norms, interfere with youths' natural development. For me, they were the best example of the old saw, *if you want a woman be a man*, and I would add, *if you want a man be a woman*. They flourished naturally around the opposite sex.

I could not help comparing Logan and Ella with my own children back in Probatis. Emily got pregnant at thirteen and Duncan became a meth addict at fifteen. In civilization, there are pressures, unrealistic expectations, and suppression of instincts that make unnatural relationships. Youth often marry for the wrong reasons, like sexual pleasure, money, or position. I thought about the promiscuity in Probatis, the many pregnant teenage girls like Emily, and the easy divorce that results in single-parent families—usually headed by a female—living in poverty. I thought about all the poor homeless youth back in civilization without families, education, or hope, procreating and perpetuating their unfortunate kind.

A perplexing contradiction occurred to me—Lilo's culture was also promiscuous, but stable and happy. He told me his wife sleeps with many men and none of his children look like him. I pondered this dilemma and recalled he had called all his children his own. Regardless of parentage, he naturally assumed the role of father for everyone. It occurred to me in civilization, we think of a marriage as exclusive, so if the spouse cheats, or if they are abandoned, the inevitable result is a single-parent family living in poverty. The problem seemed to be ownership in society compared to community in nature, which made relations between the sexes easier, more natural, and instinctual. However, it also occurred to me that possession is necessary in a complex civilization and not as necessary in a small, communal tribe.

I further thought all societies regulate sexual activity in order to provide for children, but, some society's norms are better than others, so it occurred to me the more society defers to the natural relationship between the sexes, the better. The reason to marry, for example, should be for love, which is the best environment for families. I thought this readily occurs in small, intimate natural communities, like the one Logan and Ella are in, and less often in the complex, civilized society in which Emily and Duncan grew up.

Like Logan and Ella, my relationship with Annie also flourished. And like Logan, hard work had filled me out, my skills had increased while building Halcyon, and the salt water and sun had cleansed and bronzed my skin. I was also no longer friendless. Lilo and I talked often, I was getting closer to Logan and Ella, and I was in love with Annie. Annie was a real gem—she was everything I could want in a woman. She was beautiful with her flowing red hair, had a captivating calm demeanor, a wicked sense of humor, and a body that said "Make love to me." I was enthralled.

Annie and I spent a lot of time together talking, walking and swimming. I had gained her trust and admiration and she told me I was handsome. Our relationship gradually became more physical, and one day she intimated her desire for sex with her eyes. I had just finished the bedroom so we wasted no time making love and then excitedly moved into the finished bedroom together.

Predictably, Ella and Annie quickly got pregnant. Halcyon was brimming with joy, happiness, love, and anticipation as the women's bellies swelled. Logan and I were proud, expectant fathers, and the women were radiant because they were in love and growing children. Because we were starting families, we decided to make our relationships permanent and marry, but who was going to marry us? We thought about simply exchanging vows, but this seemed illicit. Then I remembered Lilo was a tahu'a, so I asked him if he could marry us and he said he would be honored. It was a beautiful day when Ella, Link and Annie and I dressed in our formal white pareos (wrap-around skirts), and stood before Lilo to take our vows. Lilo was dressed in a flowered ceremonial robe of yellow, orange, red, and black. He recited some incomprehensible Polynesian words, and we exchanged flower leis and crowns that symbolized harmony. Lilo declared us husbands and wives and we all celebrated late into the evening.

I could not help comparing our marriages with those in civilization. My parents did not love each other. I had grown up in an angry and violent family, and my marriage to Freya was a loveless accident. In contrast, I thought our marriages were starting off on a sound, natural basis because they were based on love and the timeless laws of reproduction, children, and family. We were naturally marrying the opposite sex, unlike contrived same-sex, childless marriages in Probatis. Logan and I had started building the second bedroom, so we decided to expand it with a nursery for the children to come.

In the midst of all the happiness was one sad event. George, who was old and had lived a full life, got sick and died from cancer. It was sad watching him decline, suffer, and die. I spent a lot of time with him during his final days, recollecting our adventures together. Gracie was so distraught she also died within a few months. We created a little cemetery in the garden with headstones for George and Gracie, and Lilo conducted a solemn ceremony. I missed them terribly, but was consoled by their children and large third generations of young dogs. George and Gracie were with us in spirit through their descendants, a rambunctious pack of golden retriever puppies.

My life was tranquil on Isle de Belle with my marriage to Annie and the company of Ella and Logan; however, my mind had become bestirred. The contrast between living in nature and civilization captured my interest, so I decided to read and think about their differences in greater depth.

II. ENLIGHTENMENT AND NATURE

Chapter 12

Enlightenment

The memory of my depressing life in Probatis had faded, but not the aversion to life in a crowded city. Comparing my life then and now made me want to learn more about others' views on civilization and nature. I was full of questions like, which are the best for humans, in which are we happiest, and why? In one of my philosophy books, I read a description of Thomas Hobbes's *Leviathan*, which advocated civilization, and Jean Jacque Rousseau's *The Social Contract*, which championed nature. Both books were in my library, so I decided to read them and compare their views.

I learned a lot. Hobbes wrote that in nature, humans are naturally at war, which is a precariously violent existence. I was struck with his observation that in nature, life is solitary, poor, nasty, brutish, and short. I was reminded of my near-death experiences with savages and tigers. To avoid this and secure peace, humans form contracts between themselves, like not to kill, steal or lie. What I found particularly interesting was Hobbes's comment that for these contracts to work, humans must voluntarily limit their freedom, relinquish some natural rights, and be content with restricted liberty. However, he continued, because humans are naturally selfish and thus motivated by self-interest, these contracts and subsequent laws are insufficiently binding without force, so humans confer power on a sovereign, or Leviathan, to enforce them and bring peace.

I found an intuitive truth in Hobbes. It did seem to me that, knowing humans' violent past, many are incapable of limiting their freedom because they are egoistic. I thought it was true that humans needed authority figures to enforce their contracts, whether it was the police, courts, or Leviathan. I was struck with the thought that if humans are so selfish and Hobbes's contract is true, morality must be based on self-interest. I asked myself, why is this a problem? I asked why people obey traffic laws and concluded because they want to live. Driving on the wrong side of the road often leads to fatal, head-on collisions. I also realized that the majority in a democracy is Leviathan, which could unjustly bully the minority.

Rousseau, who championed nature, forcefully attacked Hobbes' society while touting the virtues of nature, including human nature. For Rousseau, society frustrates humans' natural impulses, demands servility, creates private property which is the source of inequality, corrupts morals, brings luxury and decay, makes people slaves to their passions, and engenders the desire to distinguish oneself, bringing about hubris, which is the root of all evil. Unlike Hobbes' *Leviathan*, humans create a political system through voluntary consent, power comes from the people, and there is a general will that is always good and concerned with the welfare of all. The stronger in society have no right to rule the weaker, so, for Rousseau, the ideal government emphasizes equality and liberty. Rousseau believed the social contract is a hoax perpetrated by the rich on the poor, Leviathan causes inequality and subservience, and force creates no rights. In nature, humans are naturally good and compassionate noble beasts who emphasize feeling over intellect, and there is no private property. Hence no inequality, and human nature is perfectible. Humans are naturally peaceful, a disposition that civilization changes to aggressiveness and which results in conflict and wars.

I found Rousseau's views appealing but simplistic and unrealistic. If human nature is perfectible, why do humans commit acts of evil in nature? If, in nature, humans enjoy liberty and independence, why am I in constant danger from savages and tigers? Sure, the stronger rule the weak in civilization, but in nature, might makes right is a fact of life. If human nature is naturally good, as Rousseau claims, why do they continually steal, fight, and murder? There were just too many flaws in Rousseau's thinking.

I came to think of reading as an essential part of my life. Learning philosophy, history, literature, politics, biographies, and science awakened my mind. I was elated with the new ideas I was learning. I began connecting the dots and seeing causes and consequences clearly, putting the present in perspective by reading about the past. The only downside was I excitedly began talking to myself to everyone's amusement.

Things were going so well for us on Isle de Belle that we decided to have a party, so we invited Lilo and his family to a luau. We built a large fire in the garden, dug a hole, and roasted a pig, and I brewed some Okolehao, or beer fermented from a plant root. Our evening eating and drinking with Lilo and his family was joyous. I was struck by how happy, fun, loving, and spontaneously affectionate they were, unlike my formerly unhappy family back in Probatis. I noticed Lilo did not resemble any of his five children, and sure enough, when he was inebriated, he offered me his wife

Louanne, which I later learned was for sex. Annie was amused and I politely declined. I showed them around the treehouse which astounded them, especially the bathroom and shower. Louanne liked the second bedroom and nursery I was just finishing, and Lilo liked the library I had just begun to frame. Louanne said she wanted Lilo to build her a house like this. Lilo and I spent a couple of hours in the library talking about my readings of Hobbes and Rousseau. He was intensely interested and said he had never lived in a city, but felt certain the slower, calmer, and peaceful life in nature is better.

My friendship with Lilo was deepening. He started calling me Kala, my Polynesian name, which was a sign of kinship. He was an interesting bundle of sometimes curious recondite knowledge. As a Shaman priest, he could talk knowledgeably about their gods, Kane, Ku, and Lono, and natural medicines, foods, and animals, but was ignorant of science, like biology, physics, and chemistry, as well as world history. At one point, Lilo said he initially did not like me because I called him a savage, but he had gotten over that long ago. He also said at first, the villagers feared me, but they are now respectful and accepting. Indeed, he said they deposed of Lucius and sent him away after he tried to kill me.

It was early evening when all hell broke loose. Lilo and I had gone down to the living room to join everyone. The sea was calm, the evening balmy, and everyone was quietly talking, eating and drinking when this incredible deafening loud bang shook the air like a large bomb going off just over us. Suddenly the ground shook violently from a powerful earthquake, and dishes, food, kindling, and glasses flew precariously through the air as the treehouse wildly shook, swayed, and whipped. Everyone grabbed something solid to keep from being tossed overboard. I learned later there had been a major underwater landslide a few miles offshore that resulted in a level-eight Richter scale earthquake, one of the most powerful for the island in recent history.

Obviously worried, Lilo shouted that an ocean earthquake, a tsunami, was coming, and that we must run to high ground immediately! With that, Lilo and his family scrambled down the stairs and ran to their canoe. They clambered aboard and began rowing home as fast as they could. I remember thinking how I hoped they make it.

Chapter 13

Tsunami

Lilo had warned us to quickly get to high ground, but I wasn't so sure. I didn't know whether we should make a run for it or stay. I looked at the thick, dense jungle, to the high ground far behind us, and then to a very pregnant Annie and Ella who would never be able to keep up. I then looked at the animals below and realized the old and young would drown because they also could not follow. I had never been much of a leader, but everyone was scared, panicky and desperately asking me what to do! So, I made a quick decision and said we would stay and make Halcyon our survival sanctuary. With that, we all immediately went to work.

Because the garden would most likely wash away, Logan and Annie ran to it and began collecting as much produce as possible. They picked all vegetables and fruits, pulled up many plants, and began hauling them to the treehouse. Ella and I quickly rounded up most of the animals, including dogs, and cajoled them up the stairs to the living room and patio. Fortunately, I had already moved all of the stash from the ship, including the books, to the treehouse. When we were done, halcyon was a crowded mass of noisy animals and produce spread throughout the living room, bedrooms, bathroom and unfinished library. Halcyon was bulging.

There was a palpable fear as an eerie silence descended, the early warning of an impending tsunami. We watched in awe as the ocean retreated out as far as we could see, exposing a vast empty sea floor strewn with rocks, coral, reefs and flopping fish. It was an unreal sight for us, being accustomed to the peaceful azure ocean, surf, and gentle waves washing ashore. Logan and I decided to take a risk, in spite of the women's fears, and try and collect some of the fish for food. We scrambled down the stairs, ran out onto the empty ocean bed, and began collecting a vast bounty of seafood.

Logan and I were so preoccupied filling our bags with fish, crabs, and clams, we failed to see the incoming wave. It was only when Logan heard the women screaming at us to run that we looked up and saw the huge, frothing wave bearing down on us. The silence had turned into a distant roar that was soon becoming a deafening roar as the wall of water approached us. We turned and ran for our lives. The wave, which was faster than us, began lapping at our heels. I thought, "Holy shit, we are going to drown!" We barely made the beach incline which slowed the tide just long enough for us to make it. We flew up the stairs and raised them just in time, to the women's great relief.

The 30-foot wave quickly flooded the lower stairs and platform,, and the fast-rising water came within 10 feet of the living room. The heavy swirling current became a violent, turbulent, boiling dark mass of debris. We watched in horror as the tsunami flattened the fence, uprooted and washed away the garden, and drowned animals.

The sapling trees were ripped from the ground, and all the animals' pens disappeared. It was depressing to watch the destruction.

The water level fluctuated for a couple of hours as the currents rushed in and out. The tide began to slowly recede to its normal level after another few hours. Stunned, we lowered the stairs and went down and walked around to look at the carnage. Fortunately, Halcyon was untouched but all of the area surrounding the tree was devastated. The fence, garden, and pens were gone and debris and dead animals were everywhere. A large part of the sandy beach had washed away and we could see flattened jungle for four to five hundred yards behind us.

When we overcame the shock of it all, we slowly led the animals down the stairs and began burying the dead ones. We were fortunate because the animals stayed together close to the tree and did not wander off. The first thing we did then was scour the area for all building materials and plants, hoping to recover as much as possible. This took some time and effort, because some of it had washed far inland. We then spent time together reimagining a new garden and animal area. We decided to greatly expand these areas by moving the larger and taller fence out about 25 feet. We had a lot of fun planning the new garden area and animal pens and were excited to begin work.

It was a long rebuilding process. Logan took charge of the garden, Ella and Annie, though very pregnant, worked on the animal shelters, and I started work on a new fence. I salvaged most of the fence posts and began setting them and stringing the wire mesh from the ship. Logan used the plants we had salvaged, along with some he found, and started recreating the garden while the women did their best to rebuild the pens and slowly fill them with pigs, chickens, cows, and sheep. It was a supremely happy and fulfilling time for all of us. We were working together to rebuild and improve Halcyon, we were in love, and we were excitedly preparing for the arrival of children.

I spent most of my time on the fence but would occasionally help Logan in the garden and Annie and Ella in the animal area. They would work, sit, rest, and then work, sit, rest because of their condition. The second bedroom was finished and Logan and Ella had already moved in, so, when I got tired of the fence, I spent time on my favorite project—the library. The siding was finished, and I was busy working on the floor-to-ceiling bookshelves. I made them and often imagined myself sitting in my easy chair surrounded by books, reading. It was to be the jewel of Halcyon and I could not wait to finish it.

My relationship with Logan was becoming almost like father and son. He treated me with great respect, unlike my children back in Probatis, and I enjoyed guiding him through some challenges like construction and his relationship with Ella. We spent a lot of time working together on various projects and caring for our pregnant wives. He flourished and I grew.

Logan surprised me one day when he asked why I read so much. He said he had watched me absorbed in books and was curious what caused such intense interest. He said he had little education, was a poor student, and never read books. I was pleased with his interest and said I have a lot of questions, like what is existence, what is real, what is consciousness, why are we here, and what we ought to do. Logan looked dumbfounded and went stone quiet. After a long silence and some stammering he asked why I ask such questions, and I said because I would rather be Socrates dissatisfied than a pig satisfied. Puzzled, Logan again went silent.

After a while Logan said these are interesting thoughts. He asked who thinks about them and I said mostly philosophers, who are the lovers of wisdom. Pensively, Logan said he sometimes wonders what makes happiness. I smiled and said philosophers have thought a lot on that question. Ancient Aristotle wrote it was a mean between extremes, Thoreau that it was to live simply, and Johnson to avoid unsatisfied desires which are like an attractive mirage that always recedes as you approach. A light went on in Logan's eyes and he asked what other questions do philosophers explore?

I was surprised by Logan's active, inquiring mind. I said they have many ideas about morality, or how we should treat one another. Aristotle thought virtue was the key, Bentham thought that morality is happiness for most, and Kant thought it was duty. They also often ask how we know what we know. Logan looked puzzled and said he knew what he knew. I smiled and asked him how he knew he was not a brain in a vat? Indeed, one famous philosopher, Socrates, believed wisdom is knowing that you don't know. Some sophists, or those who don't know, believe only faith brings true knowledge.

Finally, Logan said he was interested in what philosophers think about death. I said they have many thoughts, like Boethius, who described philosophy's ability to console those facing death. For me, because death is inevitable, when it comes you should just smile at it like an old friend who has come to take you away. Logan then asked if he could read some of my philosophy books and I said sure.

Despite the tsunami and its destruction, life on Isle Belle was good. We were alive, healthy, and happy. I realized nature was teaching me lessons. I learned that it is indifferent to me and continually offers challenges and failures. But it was also giving me strength of character, fortitude, and an optimism that surmounts its troubles. I was learning to be more tolerant and patient, and I focused on the big picture. With this new attitude, I was thinking how everything was getting better when suddenly Annie and Ella simultaneously screamed, groaned loudly, and went into labor.

Chapter 14

Healing Nature

Logan and I did as much as we could to help Ella and Annie through their labor, but birth is very much a woman's lonesome and painful task. Logan was beside himself. He had never seen a woman suffering in labor like his beloved Ella. Ella's delivery was long and dangerous. After several hours of pushing, there was no crowning, and we feared the baby had not aligned for delivery. Like her wounds from the tiger attack, we worried Ella might die. She was writhing in pain and exhausted when Logan and I decided on a seat-of-the-pants, non-medical solution, got on her stomach, pushed down, and told her to squeeze as hard as she could! With the last anguished push, a beautiful baby boy squirted out and Ella screamed a sigh of relief.

Annie's delivery was much smoother, taking only a few contractions. It was a quick delivery. The women were exhausted, Logan and I were elated, and we all celebrated the safe arrival of our children. Annie and I had a girl we bamed Sophie after Annie's mother, and Ella and Logan named their baby boy Link after me. In time, we called him Linker to avoid confusion.

With the tsunami fresh in my mind, I pondered how nature had caused such destruction, but I also realized that it was nature that repaired the damage. I started to think about nature's power to heal; not only physical injury, but also broken lives, like mine.

I recalled in society being a ridiculed untouchable, despised by all. This abuse led to my alcoholism, heartburn, and chronic headaches. My personality became abnormal, and I was always edgy, nervous, and defensive. My wife left me, my children hated me, and I had no friends. It was awful. In contrast, I thought how my idyllic time on Isle de Belle changed and healed me. It was peaceful, I exercised every day, and I worked hard on my many projects. I had a lean, healthy diet, got lots of deep sleep, and spent hours just leisurely enjoying life. At first, I was alone, so there was no one to belittle me, and later, when I became fit and strong, I attracted a beautiful young woman who loved me. Nature had erased my troubles and ushered me into the happiest time of my life.

It is unfortunate in society how boys face intense competition, physical abuse, and compelling social pressure to conform. They are expected to be strong, stoical, and fearsome. I thought it was no wonder that Logan, when he first arrived at seventeen, was withdrawn, scrawny, and spoke with a stutter. But I watched him flourish on Isle de Belle. The lack of critical contemporaries, all the hard, physical work, and total freedom changed him and allowed him to become what he is. Before my eyes, he gradually became a man; self-assured, self-directed, courageous, strong, and fierce. I remembered his standing alone, sending a fusillade of arrows into the attacking tigers, and later, his softer masculine nature, caring for Ella after her tiger attack, helping her through her difficult pregnancy and delivery, and later as his role as a loving husband and kindhearted father.

The women faced different challenges like limited opportunities and subjugation by men, which made created toxic, shrewish, waspish feminists. I thought their worst malady was to be homely. I think unattractive women face the worst human disappointments, pains, and sadness. Most are rejected by men; they have little or no sex, nobody asks them to marry, and thus, they produce no children or family. Their primal biological urge is thwarted. They live a dejected, lonely, and sad life in the shadows of society.

Annie did not have that problem because she was beautiful. Her problem in society was that her beauty defined her—everyone expected her to be the prom queen. But in nature, I noticed how she blossomed and her natural traits of calmness, cheerfulness, and resilience evolved into tranquility, joy, and fortitude. She became more than an ornament. To my delight, her natural sensuous nature became a burning desire for sex and the urge to reproduce. With the arrival of Sophie, she reached her potential, and, I think, was fulfilled.

Ella, on the other hand, *did* have that problem because she was homely. She grew up in a society that scorns ugly women. The boys did not ask her out, she had no beaus, she was ostracized, she had no chance of having children, and she was a huge disappointment to her family. She felt rejection, pain from not being welcome, agonizing disappointment with her lot in life, and deep sadness. As a result, she got fat, and developed a truculent, shrewish, complaining and angry personality, which only made her situation worse. It is no wonder that she was such an unhappy, insecure, and scared young woman when she arrived on Isle de Belle.

Ella's transformation started when she met Logan. One day I saw Logan touch her and watched her stunned reaction. She just stared at him a long time. No male had ever done that to her. We all watched with smiles as Ella steadily changed the first year. We saw that she was gradually escaping from the cruel social constructs that had been imposed upon her. She had developed a pure and accepting nature. She was working hard, caring for the animals, exercising regularly, usually by swimming in the lagoon, and frolicking and laughing with Logan. Her affection and love grew with Logan and she gradually transformed into a gorgeous young woman. The sun had given her a healthy complexion, the exercise shaped her increasingly sexy body, her eyes and personality softened, and her innate inner radiant beauty emerged in response to being loved and cherished. Her personality became beguilingly calmer with increased self-confidence. She changed to the kind of enchanting woman you just want to hug, kiss, and make love to. Personally, I think it was pretty obvious that Ella thrived being in nature around the opposite sex.

Ella's transformation made me think about society's and nature's effects on gender. In artificial Probatis, it was thought that gender is a social construct. Watching Ella's transformation showed me how wrong they are. Denying gender is like claiming that breathing is imposed upon us by society. Ella's natural feminine gender emerged and thrived in nature. Being grounded in her natural gender brought Ella a loving husband, a child, a family, and happiness. There are no Trans in nature and we are the measure of natural things rather than Man.

The repairs to Halcyon were rapidly being completed. The expanded fence was mostly built, the garden was replanted and was producing crops, and the animal pens were finished. The nursery in the second bedroom was busy with Sophie and Linker, and the library was done. I greatly enjoyed moving all my books in and started spending time sitting in my easy chair reading. Amongst my readings I was particularly intrigued with Jeremy Rifken's *Time Wars*. I found his observations on the nature of time, and in particular time in civilization and nature, trenchant. It was enlightening because I had lived in both.

It had been some time since the tiger attack and we continued to see an occasional cat prowling the fence and animal pens. We had a scare early one morning when a tiger approached as everyone was busy and the gate was open. Fortunately, Logan, alert as always, spotted him and yelled *tiger!* We all ran, closed the gate, and quickly climbed to the platform. Logan and I grabbed our bows and prepared for a fight, but the tiger just looked at us, decided it was not worth it, and left.

I often wondered what it is about civilization that oppresses. My first thought was how society is like a complex and confusing maze that challenges us with innumerable dead ends. Navigating its maze is like a pressure-filled high-wire act with potential failure at every turn. It is a human-made labyrinth of uncertainty and fear while living in the opinion of others. It is no wonder Ella was so traumatized when she first came to Isle de Belle.

After reading Jeremy Rifkin's *Time Wars,* I was convinced one of the confounding parts of the maze is faster time. Rather than amble through it at leisure, you are timed. It seems that humanity is obsessed with accelerating time. Originally, we lived within the slow rhythms of nature, but we have been speeding it up. It began with the Romans 1,500 years ago, who invented hours, and continued three hundred years ago when the Benedictine Monks invented the pendulum that brought clocks, minutes, and seconds. 200 years ago, the word 'punctuality' entered the English language, and now with computers, we measure time in nanoseconds. Back in Probatis, with the advance of technology, everything was sped up and everyone was in a hurry. With this, my experience of life became breathless and sterile and the really meaningful things like joy and love faded. I became a frozen prisoner of time. What I have found is that returning to nature has slowed time, reintroduced me to earth's rhythms, brought peace to my life, and made me relaxed and happy.

Like Logan and Ella, the healing properties of nature had changed me. I completely forgot about my awful life back in Probatis and all of the maladies I had suffered. Annie, always adoring, kept telling me I was buff and very handsome. She loved to run her hand through my long, red hair. For a scrawny guy who couldn't make the track team in high school, running down a very fast kimono dragon that was threatening the animals and killing him with my bare hands and knife felt pretty good.

My personality changed on Isle de Belle. Because life was slower, I relaxed, my blood pressure went down, and the perpetual knot in my stomach disappeared. Because I was increasingly adept at navigating the challenges of existence, my self-confidence soared. To my surprise, latent aspects of my personality slowly emerged, like undaunted courage and willfulness. I found that when I decided to pursue a difficult, sometimes dangerous goal, I invariably succeeded. Another aspect of my personality that surprised me was my happy-woman-loving-glad-to-be-alive attitude.

I also came to realize I was smarter than I thought. Having the time to pursue my daily reading was a source of pleasure and challenge. I was becoming more adept at understanding some of the esoteric intellectual conundrums in Plato's *Dialogues* and Hume's *An Inquiry Regarding Human Understanding*. I learned why we should not make an 'ought' from an 'is.' I was becoming a knowledgeable intellectual which only fueled my desire to read and learn more. Perhaps my greatest surprising enjoyment was to reflect on what I had read and develop my own unique thoughts. I had progressed from an Epicurean pig to a dissatisfied Socrates.

Even though I had forgotten about my past life, I sometimes wondered what had happened to the people I had known. Ironically, when Annie would look lovingly into my eyes and melt my heart, I found myself wondering about Freya's fate. When I watched Sophie and Linker squirming and thriving, I wondered about Emily and Duncan and what they were doing. I remembered how my city of Probatis and country of Utopianus seemed to be decaying for reasons I did not know. I decided I wanted to go back and find out. I explained my plans to Annie, Logan, Ella, and Lilo who, with reservations, wished me luck. So, I started preparing for my journey back in time.

IV.   PHILOSOPHY, NATURE, CIVILIZATION
AND HAPPINESS

Chapter 15

Decadere

My first problem was how to get to Probatis. The lifeboat I had salvaged had sunk but I remembered that Annie, Logan, and Ella had used a lifeboat to get to Isle de Belle and wondered if it was still intact. I hiked back to where I'd found them, and after a brief search, found the boat in some underbrush. I cleaned it up and was pleased to see it in seaworthy condition, with a mast for sailing. I rowed it back to Halcyon to everyone's surprise and hauled it ashore. I spent the next few weeks refurbishing and stocking the boat, including a few books, kissed Annie, said goodbye to everyone, and like I had many years ago from Astor, hoisted the sail and this time headed east into the vast blue Pacific Ocean.

I felt the same thrill of freedom and uncertain adventure sailing out into the ocean. Everything went well and I knew I was heading in the right direction, but after a couple of weeks I began getting low on food and water. I cut back on my eating, but after another week, the shortages were more acute. My clothes were shredding, I started looking like a scarecrow with very long, unkempt hair, and the boat was beginning to leak.

The lifeboat was close to sinking, when out of nowhere, this huge ocean liner appeared, came alongside, and an officer on the high bridge asked if I needed help. Grateful, I said 'yes' and they took me aboard. It was like going from the Brazilian jungle to a five-star hotel in New York. The officers were dressed in all white, pressed uniforms, and passengers were dressed to the nines. I was a curiosity—an uncivilized savage who happens to speak good English. The captain took me aside and said they were a Pacific Cruise Line ship returning to Dystopianus with 300 passengers from a cruise to Tahiti. He asked who I was and was fascinated with my story. He told a steward to get me a cabin, show me the showers, take me to the barber, get me some clothes, and bring me to dinner at five.

When I arrived, a waiter took me to the captain's table where I met some passengers. It turned out to be a philosophy-themed cruise, and most passengers were philosophy students and professors. They quickly took an interest in my life in nature on a tropical island. They became even more interested when I told them about Lilo, that I was returning to Probatis, and had read Hobbes and Rousseau's views, which precipitated a lively discussion comparing civilization and nature. Professor Hobes said civilization is best because nature is brutish, and Professor Ersmus emphasized the importance of religion in society. The conversation became contentious when a student, Horace Dogenes, asserted the importance of self-sufficiency in nature.

Professor Rousset emphatically claimed the noble beast in nature is the highest form of human development, and Professor Spinza derided the dogmatically oppressive religions of society. The debate became heated and was only cooled when Professor Albert Lakaso, a free thinker, said the contrast is pointless because we all inhabit another transcendent realm beyond experience, and Professor Bill Boeths said it does not matter because we all die and in the end become nothing, which made professor Lakaso cringe.

My head was spinning with metaphysical philosophic thoughts when I returned to my cabin. My interest in the issue, however, was stoked with my reading that evening. I started Malthus' *An Essay Concerning Human Population* and Johnathan Swift's *Gulliver's Travels* in which he used Flappers to waken silly metaphysical philosophers. I also started reading Heather MacDonald's *When Race Trumps Merit* and learned about disparate impact, reverse discrimination, and racial double standards.

When we docked, I said goodbye to everyone, took a bus to Probatis, and was shocked as I drove into the city. It looked like a war zone with ugly graffiti everywhere, a sea of tents, and decrepit vagrants and beggars. It only got worse downtown. Garbage, human waste, and needles were everywhere. Stooped, deranged, comatose drug addicts lined the sidewalks. It looked like a waste-land with plywood storefronts everywhere because businesses had fled the city. The infrastructure was crumbling with pot-holed streets, broken-up sidewalks and blank traffic lights. I was dismayed. Probatis looked like an empty, dead, ghost town. I asked the bus driver what happened and he just shrugged and said Probatis is now called Decadere and the former country of Utopianus is no longer. It is now called Dystopianus.

The bus dropped me off at a downtown YMCA and I checked in. When I got to my room, I couldn't believe the conveniences I had long forgotten. I flipped a switch and turned on lights, turned a dial and got cold or hot air, opened a refrigerator door and got ice, turned a handle and got clean fresh water, and pushed a lever and my bodily waste disappeared. I marveled how society dwellers take these conveniences for granted.

I had no old friends to look up, but I did have family. I decided to try to find my mother first. I found the decrepit house we had lived in and knocked on the door. A young woman answered and said she had never heard of Olivia Lawrence. I found a nearby computer café and conducted a search with the help of the waitress. It produced three matches, one of whom had an extensive criminal record of drug abuse and was about my mother's age. I found her in a government-run nursing home for the poor.

It was an unsettling experience seeing mom for the first time after so many years. It was sad because I did not love her as she had abused me when I was young. In trepidation, I went to her room and was shocked at her appearance. She was old, stooped, wrinkled, and enfeebled after years of drugs, and unable to sit up. My body went tense as my mind was flooded with bad memories.

She just stared at me and asked who I was. I said I was her son, Link, and she said she thought I drowned. I felt no emotional connection with my mother and decided to leave. Just as I was walking out the door, she surprised me and said, Malcolm, my father, had died long ago from alcoholism. She asked if I would like to see his grave, or would like the addresses of my sisters and former wife, Freya. I said I would, and she wrote them down. I then thanked her and left. I learned later that she died shortly after my visit.

I didn't go to my father's grave but was curious to see my sisters. I took the bus to their apartment, knocked on the door, and Mede answered. My first thought was that Mede and Mopper were much older and uglier than I remembered. They were marginally civil. Mede was still the virulent anti-male feminist, and Mopper was a super haughty, arrogant prig. I was not surprised to learn they both had divorced twice, were childless, and were still full of spite and anger. I could not wait to get out of there. While leaving, I felt lucky for having escaped their evil Medusan embrace.

My first feeling when I saw Freya was deep sorrow. I found her dirty apartment. She answered the door, and said with a broad smile, "*Link,*" which quickly turned to fear when a booming voice yelled "*Who is that?*" from a back room. She was teary, had deep, dark bags under her eyes, was emaciated, and covered with bruises. She was a druggie, like her mother, living with an abusive drug dealer. We talked for a bit. She said I had changed and grown into a strong, handsome, and articulate man. She said she was happy for me. Her submissive, downcast, almost contrite behavior saddened me somehow.

It was just then that the skinny man appeared and hit her in the face for not answering him. She cowered, I grabbed him by the throat, hoisting him in the air. As he gasped for breath, I said "*If you ever hit her again, I will beat you to a pulp!*" I dropped him and he ran off. Freya, amazed and relieved, thanked me profusely. I was pleasantly surprised at my strength. I also realized I never felt the need to intimidate and threaten another human in nature. I felt grateful I had escaped civilization long ago and thought if I had stayed I probably would have ended up like Freya. I hugged poor, trembling Freya, and as I was leaving, she handed me a paper with our children's telephone numbers. Freya died a year later.

Both Emily and Duncan were surprised when I called, said they would like to see me, and suggested a nearby restaurant. It was a surprisingly happy reunion, reconnecting and filling in our pasts. Duncan was married and had a son, and Emily was divorced and had two daughters. They were most curious about my story, so I described being adrift at sea, the shipwreck, Isle de Belle and the treehouse, the tiger and savages attacks, finding Ann, Logan, and Ella, and our marriages and children. I described the garden, animals, ocean, and lagoon where we swam. They were enraptured with my life and amazed at how I had changed. They said I was not as they remembered me. Duncan, who used to hate me, said it sounded like paradise, and Emily, who used to treat me with contempt, said she wanted to go back with me. Both said they were amazed that I had become such a strong, confident and educated person. The reunion made me think that there does exist a certain transcendental bond between parents and their offspring.

We were enjoying ourselves so much that we decided to move to the restaurant's bar and continue our conversation. As we walked in,

I saw the bus driver, who smiled and waved us over to his table. We sat down. He said his name was Joe, and I introduced my children. With that, we began what was perhaps the most enlightening discussion about how Probatis became Decadere.

I began by saying I could not believe the decay and destruction of Probatis; that it looked like one of Salvador Dali's surreal paintings. Joe said it all began when the progressive socialists took over. Their mantra was *soak the rich*, which they did with exorbitantly high taxes. Predictably, the rich—and the businesses they own—left. Go to the street Enterprise Way in our capitalistic neighbor city, Lake Harmony, to see where they all went. Their parking lots are packed, and office buildings are filled with our businesses. Compare this with Decadere's empty downtown. Because the city's tax revenue declined, the socialists incurred debt and began cheating. They started raiding other sources of revenue like the water and street maintenance funds, which precipitated the decay of our sewers, water lines, streets, and sidewalks.

Duncan said the streets in Decadere are not vacant, but rather full of needy, unkempt, homeless people. We used to call them bums, hobos and vagrants, but the liberal socialists thought this was demeaning and started calling them homeless and now unhoused. You can change the name, but the reality remains. We also used to have vagrancy and loitering laws that mitigated the problem, but the socialists rescinded those laws, which is why we have such a vagrant problem today.

Joe then said the vagrancy problem is just a consequence, whereas the cause of the problem was the devaluation of police and the

District Attorney's unwillingness to prosecute criminals. He said a few years ago the city council decided racism was more important than safety and started defunding the police because they thought it was racist. The smaller, demoralized police force stopped enforcing many laws, and crime naturally skyrocketed. To make matters worse, our then progressive socialist District Attorney stopped prosecuting some crimes because she thought rehabilitation was better than retribution. Because there were no consequences for wrongdoing, crime increased even more. The blinkered District Attorney never read Seneca who wrote that the purpose of retributive justice is to punish the wrongdoer, act as a deterrent, and remove the dangerous criminals from society. She failed miserably on all three counts.

Duncan then said these are the reasons we have so much violence today. Some are property crimes like graffiti, burglary, and carjacking and others are against people. Nightly shootings, murders, and gang warfare have destroyed our peace, ruined our community spirit, and left swaths of empty no man's land. Emily, who had been quiet much of the time, said much of the violence is political with extremist right supremacist White Boys that fight extreme left Marxist black-clad youth. Much of this is fueled by our out-of-control bored youth that riot and tear down historic city statues. She said it makes me angry to think how our political leaders and police did nothing last year to prevent this wanton violence and destruction. They should have called out the National Guard.

Emily continued and said the teachers supported by their all-powerful unions only threw gas on the conflagration. In their classrooms, teachers began promoting ideological leftist agendas like socialism, critical race theory, and LGBTQ+. They championed the idea that human nature is a social construct, so transgenderism and same-sex marriage are normal. They taught our children never to use pronouns like 'him' and 'her.' This infuriated parents like me who threatened to take their children out of school. The teachers' response was for their unions to pressure the politicians to pass laws that prohibited schools from sharing information on pupils with their parents so they would not know what their children are being taught. This was like propaganda in a collectivist communist country, and not free Utopianus.

Emily then said that she once took a philosophy class and learned about the assassins' creed which is, if nothing is true, everything is permitted. In Probatis, there were certain foundational truths, but they hindered the liberal socialists' agenda, so they began saying everything is relative. With this, nothing was true, and moral decadence began. We got naked bike rides, celebrated drag shows, and unlimited sexual practices. Probatis lost its moral compass and became Decadere.

It had been a stimulating conversation, Joe said goodbye, and I told Duncan and Emily I was leaving in a few days. We hugged goodbye and I left. Walking away, I could not help but recall the many stressed, long, and unhappy faces I had seen during my visit compared to the bright and happy faces of my family back on Isle de Belle. I was glad to be going home.

Chapter 16

Return to Isle de Belle

I was excited about going home, but unsure how to get there. I went to a busy port and asked if anyone was going to Polynesia who needed a deck hand. I was discouraged because there were none, but fortuitously, I saw a poster for Pacific Cruise Lines and thought the ship that picked me up just might be going back. I hitchhiked to their port and was encouraged to see the same ship docked. I went to their offices and learned it was preparing to leave on its round-trip cruise to Tahiti. I had no money, so I asked if they needed any hands. Just then, the captain walked by, saw me, and exclaimed "Link, what are you doing here?" I explained my situation, and he said, "Grab your bag and come with me! We need a cabin boy." I climbed aboard and the ship departed, heading out into the vast Pacific Ocean.

I worked cleaning cabins, slept in the crews' dorm, and ate in the crew cafeteria for three weeks. I got to know many of the young crew members, like Evan, who had just graduated from college, and Julie, who was escaping a bad marriage. I was struck with the civilization-like class stratification on the ship with first class, second class, steerage, and the crew at the bottom. It was like living in luxury while wearing a straitjacket. This was in stark contrast to the nature-like balmy nights on the ocean when I would stand at the railing alone, absorb nature, and enjoy existence.

My everyday experience on the ship got interesting one day when the captain invited me to his table for dinner, where I was surprised to see Professors Hobes and Rousset, who I had met on the first cruise. They were genuinely happy to see me and, knowing my background, were curious about my experience in Decedare. Professor Rousset asked how it went and I told them about overpopulation, the druggies, homelessness, violence, hunger, and unhappy people. They were particularly interested in the hardships of my old family. Professor Rousset said this is the problem in civilization—it brings the Malthusian trap. I had read some of Malthus' book but could not remember it all so I asked him what that was. He said that Thomas Malthus was a 19th century English economist who wrote *An Essay on the Principle of Population* in which he noted that even though increased food production could bring improvement, it was temporary because it leads to population growth. He said all you get is more population and the need for more food. The more need you feed, the more need you get, to which Professor Hobes cited the Biblical observation that the poor will always be with you.

Then Professor Rousset said nature has no similar problem because populations stay small due to Darwin's survival of the fittest. He said Rousseau, an ancestor of mine, in his *Social Contract,* glorified nature and envisioned the perfect man or Noble Beast. Rousseau believed civilization corrupts humans and fosters greed. However, there are some problems with Malthus' theory, said Professor Hobes, in that it does not account for increased food production due to the Industrial Revolution, and it does not explain the effect of increasing deaths with more people.

Professor Lakaso, who had not said much, then pointed out that the Malthusian trap leads to the Malthusian Catastrophe which is when the lower classes suffer from war, famine, and disease, which in the case of Decadere is violence, hunger, and drugs. This, he added, is what ruined your family. The ultimate cause, he added, is increasing population due to socialism's 'to each his need.' With that, the conversation became an unintelligible flurry of intellectual jargon. After a while, I thought these ungrounded metaphysical philosophers needed Swift's Flapper to smack them back into reality.

Their conversation caused me to think about the conflict back in Decadere and civilization in general. It occurred to me that Malthus and Rousseau represented two common and timeless world views. For Malthus, humans are selfish, human nature is constant, and society is not perfectible, whereas for Rousseau, humans are altruistic, human nature is improving, and society *is* perfectible. I realized these two different visions are probably the source of most human contention and strife in society.

I was inclined to think that Malthus was right and nature is more conducive to human felicity. On the other hand, I knew life had been good in early Utopianus, and wondered why Probatis in

Utopianus had become Decadere in Dystopianus. Intellectually, I was confused, but emotionally, all was quite clear—I was glad to have escaped civilization and elated to be going home.

After dinner, I went back to my bunk and started reading the last two books I brought. Tocqueville's *Democracy in Utopianus* explained much about democracy in Probatis and its decline due in part to the tyranny of the majority. I also began re-reading Utopianus' *Declaration of Independence, Constitution*, and *Bill of Rights*. I was reminded of the lofty ideals of justice and equality, and dismayed by how Decadere had wandered so far from its profound, historic roots. Both books explained much of what the philosophers had said at dinner.

As time passed, I found myself thinking more about home. My trip to Decadere had satisfied my curiosity about my past city and family. I recalled after a few months on Isle de Belle how I found myself living joyously and how I could not wait to live my new life. The last few nights on the boat railing, I thought only of home, returning to that simple life, and seeing Annie, my daughter, and those I love. My anticipation was overwhelming.

The day of our arrival, I kept scanning the horizon and felt pure exhilaration when Isle de Belle appeared in the distance. As the ship got closer, I saw the tree, and slowly, my beloved Halcyon came into view. I was beside myself with joy. It was when the ship anchored that I saw everyone—Annie, Logan and Ella with Sophie and Linker—running down to the beach elated and wildly waving their arms. I scrambled into the lowered tender and we motored to the beach. I jumped out and ran into Annie's arms and kissed her profusely. She felt really good, looked lovingly in my eyes, smiled, and said *I love you.* I then hugged Sophie, embraced Logan, Ella, and Linker, and patted the giddy goldens. It was a glorious reunion. The first thing I did was go to the lagoon, strip, and swim. The second thing was to take Annie into the bush and make passionate love.

Back at Halcyon, I saw the now mature garden and the many animals and made a nostalgic tour. The living room looked warm and inviting and my library beckoned me to sit and read. That evening, there were many questions, so I told them about the cruise ship, Decadere, Freya, my sisters, and children, Emily and Duncan. They said everything went fine after I left but they all missed me. They said they were getting worried about me after a few weeks but were happily astonished when the cruise ship appeared. Sophie and Linker earnestly tried to join the conversation but could only babble.

The library was so inviting I began spending more time there. I could not help but ponder the many things I had learned about nature and civilization. I thought about what sad things had happened to my old family, the decay of the city I had grown up in, my experience on Isle de Belle, the philosophers' conversations, and my readings. I had a lot to think about.

Chapter 17

Link on Nature and Civilization

I was happy to be home, to hold Annie, catch up with Logan and Ella, play with Sophie and Linker, and watch the throng of exuberant golden retrievers. They reminded me of George and Gracie and the good times I'd had with them. As you would expect, Annie and Ella quickly got pregnant, and we started planning for our soon-to-be new arrivals. My return was made more joyous when Lilo and his family arrived, and we all drank, ate, talked, laughed, and danced.

I could not help but think about civilization and nature. I had read much on the topic and had extensive experience growing up in civilization and now living in nature. My trip to Decadere had been a shock. I wondered how it was that stable Probatis had become chaotic Decadere. I asked Lilo sitting next to me whether humans are happier in civilization or nature and his answer was conditional. He said he understandably prefers nature, but he did not know enough about civilization to make an intelligent comparison. A storm was gathering outside, and the sky was turning gray. It began to rain, and the family gathering was joyously loud, so I suggested we grab some Okolehao beers and go to the library to talk. Lilo said it was a grand idea and we left the party for the library.

We climbed up to the library, built a warm fire, settled into the comfortable easy chairs with a beer in our hands, and began a ranging discussion on civilization, nature, and happiness, while rain fell outside. I began by contrasting Hobbes and Rousseau's views on human nature, ethics, and civilization. I then asked Lilo if he thought humans were noble beasts. Lilo thought a minute and said he was not sure if humans are noble, but in his society, if they are brave, compassionate, and in time, wise, they are good.

I said it occurred to me that humans' original state is one mostly alone in nature. Sure, we have parents, perhaps siblings and relatives, and often a few neighbors. This seems natural to me. But after observing Decadere, I wonder if large numbers of humans living together generates civilization, the development of which brings certain inevitable and possibly fatal consequences.

I continued by saying that this is not an easy question because both have so many advantages and disadvantages. Indeed, it seems every advantage has a disadvantage. Civilization has medicine, conveniences, and culture on the one hand, but crowding, pollution, and class hierarchies on the other. Nature is calm, pristine, and free on one hand but has no modern medicine, no education, and isolation on the other. It is complex because, for example, civilization is safe with Leviathan but dangerous with crime, and nature is safe from crime but full of dangerous animals, like the tigers that attacked us. Indeed, both can be stable or unstable, restful or stressful, social or lonely, secure or fearful, and predictable or precarious. It seems that choosing which is 'better' is a personal decision. If you had a happy childhood as a rich aristocrat, you might well prefer civilization, but if you had a miserable childhood as a pauper, you might prefer nature. Much depends on how much you gain or lose in both environments.

This said, I do think that civilization has the tendency to alter, corrupt, and magnify the simple ways of nature. It presents more problems than it solves. Lilo, who was obviously intrigued, asked what problems.

The first is rule by the people. Democracy, for example, is a good ideal, but an abstract and protean political system that sometimes detaches citizens from traditions, customs, and historic roots. Past successful ways are often ignored. Democracy also brings De Tocqueville's tyranny of the majority. The minority has little say. Rule by the people also often brings extreme demagogic politicians as the moderate Solons are sidelined. I noticed in Decadere the melting pot philosophy, which was a cohesive force, gave way to diversity, which is divisive. The consequence was less societal cordiality and increased class antagonisms. Lilo said their chiefdom is a simple system with deep roots and homogeneity. However, like your democracy, we do occasionally get extremist chiefs who punish protesters, but we usually depose them.

Another problem, I continued, is the corruption of human's natural sexuality in civilization. The timeless reasons for sex have been to procreate, and to support the children in families. What I saw in Decadere was disturbing with the diminution of genders, the celebration of alternate sexual practices like homosexuality, and untold hidden artificial standards for love, marriage, sex, and reproduction. Lilo looked perplexed. He said in his culture, there were no artificial sexual constructs. It is purely natural, and everyone is happy.

Just as I began describing the problem of violence in Decadere, the clouds suddenly turned dark gray, the wind began whipping, and the rain became a torrent as darkness descended upon us. Lilo said it was not a tsunami, but close to it. So, Lilo and I got another beer, closed the shutters, threw a log on the fire, and continued our conversation.

In my neighborhood, growing up in Decadere, there were violent gangs and drug dealers, and on my visit back I saw nightly riots, daily shootouts, and murders. It seems to me that when humans congregate, they naturally fight, so violence is endemic to civilization. Decadere's ironic response was to defund police, stop prosecuting criminals, and eliminate capital punishment, which only made matters worse. Amused Lilo responded and said there is also violence in nature. We have tribal wars, robbery, cannibalism, murder, and infanticide, as well as many lethal animals that kill. If there are noble savages in nature, they are just as capable of hating their neighbor as anyone else. It occurs to me the real problem is human nature and not civilization.

One of the biggest problems in Decadere is the corruption of morals. It is like they abandoned universal principles and made humans the measure of all things. As a consequence, results have become more important than intentions and a plethora of strict liability laws have ensued. It has become a kind of morality in which nothing is true, so everything, from drugs to sexual practices, is permitted. This has naturally led to capricious and relative utilitarianism, or happiness for the most. They abandoned Hobbes' social contract and the golden rule which are the true sources of morality. They learned too late that their new free-floating morality only brings problems and their typical response is *we are not far enough downstream*, or it just needs more time. The problem is they are never *far enough downstream* because the moral utopia they envision does not exist.

Lilo laughed and said they have a more primitive morality with unwritten social contracts enforced by 'might makes right.' Because our villages are small, there is no anonymity, which makes it difficult to escape the contracts. However, he continued, we do have some of your Protagoras because of an occasional capricious chief.

I was surprised to see downtown Decadere a wasteland with plywood storefronts. I was told socialism and its high taxes had driven the businesses away. The result had been a larger population dependent on a shrinking, debt-ridden government with less tax revenue. I was told that nobody starts a business in Decadere, and if they do, it quickly fails in a sea of drug addicts because they all drugs were now perfectly legal. You would think the educators would sound the alarm on decaying society, but the schools had become the vehicle for indoctrination and not enlightenment.

With that, one shutter blew open, and driving rain began pouring in. Lilo and I just closed the shutter, barricaded the door, threw a log on the fire, got another beer, and continued our conversation.

One of the most depressing developments in Decadere is the alteration and abandonment of the original cherished ideals of life, liberty, justice, and equality. Liberty has become security through collectivism, equality has become equal in all respects, and justice has become free-floating social justice. Decaderians have sold their soul to the devil for comfort, advantage, and a little bread. Lilo just chuckled. He said that my ideals sounded good, lofty, and unreal. In nature, there are no guarantees of life, liberty, justice, or equality. Nature is indifferent to these human ideals.

The ethos, I continued, of early Probatis of individualism and industry has been corrupted and now its zeitgeist embraces collectivism and other-reliance. Ironically, I think it is civilizations' successes that are the source of its decline. It is its own worst enemy. One example is the previously mentioned advent of democracy, where the people rule. Democracy brings the freedom humans want, but in Decadere, they misused it through excess and indulgence. The problem is exacerbated by civilizations' specialization of labor and the efficiencies and abundance it brings. Abundance, wealth, and plenty are sometimes the Petri dish of corruption and decadence. Lilo again chuckled and said with a smirk that if he lived in such abundance, he would lie around and make love to women all day.

It is efficiency and abundance that brought decline to early prosperous Probatis. They detached humans from nature which in time thwarted Darwin's survival of the fittest and brought the overpopulation Thomas Malthus described. It was like a snowball growing in size as it rolls. Progressive policies fed need and only got more need. The inevitable results were crowding, traffic, and pollution. What I described, said Lilo, sounded ominous. He said they don't have those problems because nature keeps the population small.

It was the middle of the night when we paused our conversation and congratulated each other on our wisdom and insight. It seemed the more beer we drank, the smarter we got. We also noticed how the library had begun swaying in the wind. The raging storm outside seemed to symbolize the troubles of civilization. We decided to continue our conversation. Lilo got us two more beers, I stoked the fire, and we settled back into our easy chairs and picked up where'd we left off.

One of the central reasons for civilizations' problems is their inclination to complexity. Its fast nature alters time. It accelerates it, hurries humans, and detaches them from nature's natural rhythms. City denizens are always rushing, multi-tasking, and frazzled while suffering nervous exhaustion and heartburn due to compressed time. Their hyped existence is made worse when they are forced by conventions and laws to navigate civilization's complex labyrinth with its layers of rewards and punishments. This unnatural maze deforms humans and their emotions, beliefs and experiences. Love becomes lust, freedom becomes security, and competition becomes hate. Its artificial cities, in which everything is thought possible, become stinking cesspools of corruption and debauchery that deny timeless human nature.

Nature, on the other hand, is easier to navigate because it is simpler. There are no complex labyrinths. Its villages are small, simple, natural, and free. Even your illusionary primitive religion satisfies your curiosity and calms you. I think there is something to be said for Erasmus' observation that 'ignorance is bliss.'

Lilo then said that, like Thoreau, he prefers his small simple society. He said it occurs to him that when humans start tinkering with nature, as they do in civilization, it only brings many of the problems I described. The invention of the internal combustion engine, for example, brought conveniences, but also pollution and global warming.

In pondering our topic, are humans happier in civilization or nature, I can't help recalling Thomas Hobbes and Jean Jacque Rousseau. It occurs to me that Hobbes' view is intuitively right, but he failed to envision the consequences of civilization that I have described, like overpopulation, faster time, complicated existence, and artificial structure. He seems to be describing the ideal political state for humans and not the naturally best one. On the other hand, although unrealistic, Rousseau seems to describe the happiest natural state of humans, or that in simple nature. Like Alan Mooreheads' *Noble Savage*, Rousseau's is happily simple, unsophisticated, and naked. His life may be solitary, poor, nasty, brutish and short, but it is a happy one. Lilo smiled and said, "Look, Link, the wind and rain have stopped, and it's beginning to clear."

I continued and said, "Just compare the traits of humans in civilization and nature. In civilization, they are suspicious, often prevaricate, inclined to resist work, seek pleasure, are avaricious, and idealistic dreamers. In nature, they are usually trusting, forthright, industrious, stoic, sharing, and realistic. Many civilizations' self-righteous know-better-than-you leaders advance strange unconstrained visions like same-sex marriage, disparate impact, affirmative action, Critical Race Theory, socialism and Marxism, LGTBQ+, drag shows for children, and transgenderism. They are the culprits who sow the seeds of civilization's eventual decay and destruction, like in Decadere. Lilo looked puzzled and said that he didn't know what disparate impact, Critical Race Theory, or LGTBQ+ were, but they sounded like a poisonous toad.

I said compare his life back in Decadere and now. Clotho's predestined life of pain is now a bright future; nasty people like Mede, Moppen, and Freya have been replaced by loving Annie and my daughter Sophie; I need less and have fewer wants; I can easily take care of my family; I fish, farm, and hunt rather than clean toilets; Logan, Annie, and Ella respect me; my physical body has become buff and strong; my happiness has extinguished any mental angst; I am successful in most areas of life; and I am no longer ignorant; rather, I am educated and enlightened. Best of all is my busy and robust sex life. Nature has undone and healed what civilization did to me.

It occurs to me that happiness comes from the people we surround ourselves with. You can live among negative, angry, unhappy people, or positive, friendly, warm, and happy people, like you. I told Lilo I think he is the kind of human that naturally occurs in nature away from civilization; that is the Noble Beast. Lilo said he was not so sure about being noble, but agreed wholeheartedly that true happiness comes from people.

Lilo, I told him, I am just happier here on golden Isle de Belle living in nature. I just feel good here. I like the balmy weather, being close to the jungle and sea, living simply with my family, and being close to naturally, healthy, happy, simple, amiable, and joyful people like you. To me it is the idyllic existence.

With that, the wind and rain stopped, it began clearing, and Lilo and I got up and went outside to enjoy the glorious, sunny, beautiful, and warm morning. It was like a new day. We had talked all night and were intellectually and physically exhausted. I told Lilo I was no longer confounded, but rather now realized, in spite of civilization's advantages, nature is better. Lilo smiled and told me he was glad I'd decided to stay. It seems to me our conversation was a lot of puzzling about nothing.

Chapter 18

Felicity

A few days after my marathon talk with Lilo, I found myself alone, lying on the crest of the beach under the tree, the same place I had lain when I was first shipwrecked, admiring the vast blue ocean. I felt contentedly happy and free. I began to reminisce about my new life on Isle de Belle. I thought about my grand life adventure adrift on the ocean and shipwreck on a tropical island struggling to survive.

I recalled at first feeling marooned and desperately wanting to return home, but as time passed, I came to realize my new verdant home was paradise. It was environmentally pristine, rich in animals and vegetation, watered, and warm. To survive, I got to work, and recalled salvaging the ship, starting the garden, building animal pens, and planning the treehouse. It did not take long for me to want to stay. I also thought about the many dangers I had faced, including almost drowning, the dangerous animals, the vicious savages, and the tsunami. The danger had enlivened and energized me. My life was no longer commonplace and dull.

I thought about the fascinating books I had read and the new ideas I learned. I enjoyed doing a mental survey of my favorite authors, Tolstoy, Epictetus, Emerson, Spinoza, Cicero, and Swift. I wasn't sure what to think about Bowman. Above all, I thought about the people I met and loved. My love affair with Annie, friendships with Logan and Ella, and growing attachment to Sophie and Linker. Because Annie and Ella were pregnant again, I also thought about our growing family. I remembered my loyal golden retriever, George, and his mate, Gracie, and all the grand adventures we had together. I thought how fortunate I was to be enjoying their descendants.

I smiled, remembering my first encounter with the savage Lilo, how we had become friends, and our many engaging conversations about life, survival, faith, purpose, and meaning. I was fortunate to have known a true human of nature. We would talk endlessly about what constitutes happiness. Some prescriptions were from others, like make the world a place that brings you joy, live simply, don't fight time and nature, have courage to avoid living in fear and trembling, and your happiness is in proportion to what you do not want. I think the best prescriptions were from our experiences, like to love, appreciate family, and live life now.

It was heaven lying under the tree listening to the ocean, unencumbered, free, and happy when Lilo and his large family arrived and stirred me from my reminiscing slumber. We all went up to the living room where Annie and Ella had been busy cooking dinner and had a joyous holiday gathering, eating, drinking, talking, singing, laughing, and dancing. Logan and I brought out our pipes and began a rousing Sir Marcus' *Highland Fling* while Annie and Ella danced. Of course, Linker and Sophie did their best to imitate us. Lilo and I just looked at each other and thought, *this is the stuff of happiness.*

I was elated to be back. I felt like I had returned to my true home. I thought if I had a time machine and could return to any point in my life, this would be the time.

Thanks for reading my story, I hope you liked it.

Link Zamperini Irwin Spinoza Lawrence, a.k.a. Ikaika Kala Hana

OTHER BOOKS BY JOHN L. BOWMAN

Reflections on Man and the Human Condition
Selected Topics in Philosophy
Nobody's Perfect
How to Succeed in Commercial Real Estate
Socialism in America
God's Lecture
A Reader's Companion
Stoicism, Enkrasia and Happiness
Aegean Summer
The Art of Volleyball Hitting
Graduate School
Provocative and Contemplative Quotations
On Law
A Reference Guide to Stoicism
A Reader's Companion II
Democracy and Why It Will Fail in America
Philosophy and Happiness
My Travels (unpublished)
How to Get Rich
A Reader's Companion III
On Humans
I Knew This Would Happen
Tupac
The Plague
Eros
The Death of Oscar Uzgalis